"I want you off my ranch,"

she said.

He stepped closer, careful not to touch her.

"I'm not leaving, Amanda. I'm sorry as hell for what I said. I know I have the devil's temper and it gets me in more trouble than it should. But I'm not going. Forgive me, sugar."

"I'm not your sugar." On that her voice did break, just a little. "And I want you off the ranch. There's nothing for you here."

"I'm starting to think you're wrong on that. I think there's a lot here for both of us, if we just see where it'll lead us." With that, he took a step closer and pressed his lips against hers, drawing her into his arms.

MARRY ME, Cowboy

BOSS LADY AND THE HIRED HAND

Barbara McMahon

Kids & Kin

Silhouette Books

Published by Silhouette Books
America's Publisher of Contemporary Romance

SILHOUETTE BOOKS

ISBN 0-373-65343-3

BOSS LADY AND THE HIRED HAND

Copyright © 1997 by Barbara McMahon

Printed in U.S.A.

BARBARA McMAHON

International bestselling author Barbara McMahon has
been writing for over two decades for Harlequin and
Silhouette. More than seven million copies of her
books have sold in 37 different countries in 20
different languages. Many of the more than 50 books
she's written have a cowboy theme—not surprising
since she lives in California. There's nothing like
a rugged cowboy falling in love. Still, Barbara likes
to alternate with stories set in big cities—like
San Francisco—where she lived for many years before
moving to the Sierra Nevada Mountains. For other
books by Barbara McMahon, visit her Web site:
www.barbaramcmahon.com. Happy reading!

Please address questions and book requests to:
Silhouette Reader Service
U.S.: 3010 Walden Ave., P.O. Box 1325, Buffalo, NY 14269
Canadian: P.O. Box 609, Fort Erie, Ont. L2A 5X3

To Cristine Grace:
Thanks—let's do one hundred!

One

Hawk Blackstone paused in the doorway to the diner and surveyed the place carefully before stepping inside. Old habits died hard. Of course, it was usually bars and honky-tonks that needed care. But he always liked to know who was in a place, and the location of all the exits. His sweep absorbed the assortment of citizens in the booths, at the scattered tables and along the counter. The mix was the same as in most towns he'd lived in: cowboys, ranchers, businessmen, a woman or two. Nothing distinguished this diner from hundreds of others.

He headed for the counter, grimacing at the stab of pain in his ribs. The service was usually better there and he could watch the waitresses as they worked. Beat sitting alone at a table.

There were four empty seats, two each between diners. He chose the one next to the only female sitting on the high stools. An old man read the paper on the seat beyond. Flicking her a quick glance, his eyes moved on. He eased onto the padded seat and reached for the menu. His movements were slow, giving in to the ache in his muscles. As his hand grasped the menu, he suppressed a wince. Damn, his fingers hurt. Bruised and skinned, they were a mute testimony to yesterday's fight. What a damn fool way to celebrate his thirtieth birthday, a knockdown drag-out fight. When was he going to outgrow that instinctive reaction to wade in with his fists and ask questions later?

"What does the other guy look like?" A bright, perky waitress with flaming red hair stopped before him and shoved a cup of coffee across the width of the counter. Her smile was friendly.

"Worse than me," Hawk acknowledged. He smiled back, feeling the pull against his swollen jaw. One day he'd learn to control his blasted temper, he vowed, as he had hundreds of times before. It took longer and longer each time to recover from the fights. Hell, maybe he was just getting old.

Thirty. Damn, he couldn't believe he had just turned thirty. He didn't like it but there wasn't anything he could do about it. And what did he have to show for his thirty years on this earth? No place to call home. Friends scattered to the four winds. Some money in the bank.

He felt, rather than saw, the girl next to him glance his way. Slowly he turned toward her. She was a pretty little thing, he noted. Despite his interest in filling up the hollow in his stomach, he took the time to study her. He wasn't that old yet. Of course she was as young as could be, but it couldn't hurt to look.

She had drawn her hair into a long braid that hung down her back. It was the rich color of a chestnut horse. He knew in the sunlight it would gleam with hidden fire. Her eyes were a wary gray, fringed by lashes so dark he almost wondered if she'd dipped into hoof black. Her skin had been recently burned by the sun and peeled just a little across her nose. It made her look even younger. He smiled, ready to start a conversation, but she looked away quickly.

"What'll you have?" The waitress claimed his attention.

Hawk ordered, then sipped his hot coffee. The girl beside him ate steadily. Odd, a girl alone so early in the morning. Idly he wondered who she was and why she was in the diner at this hour all alone. Sliding another glance in her direction, he took in the faded work shirt and worn jeans. He couldn't see her feet without giving away his perusal, but he knew she wore boots. Nothing else would fit. Hooked on the back of her stool was a dusty Stetson.

He tipped his own hat back and looked away. Maybe she was the daughter of one of the ranchers, waiting for her dad. None of his business who she was or why she was here. Too young for him, even if he were interested. He liked them old enough to vote.

After he filled up, he planned to head for the local feed store and check out any job listings. That fight had not only bruised his hands and body, it had ended his employment at the Circle J. Fifth time in four years a fight had gotten him fired. Would he ever learn to control his blasted temper? To celebrate his birthday, he'd gotten knee-walking drunk and then took offense to Jason Johnson's snide remarks. He should have picked on someone else instead of the boss's son.

He took another sip of coffee. What was done was done. He needed to find a new job. Maybe here in Tagget, Wyoming, maybe not. If there was nothing available, he'd move on.

"Here you go, cowboy. Holler if you want anything else." The waitress plopped down the loaded plate and slipped the bill beneath the edge. With a quick refill for his cup, she moved down the counter to see to another arrival.

"Pass the salt, please," Hawk said to the girl beside him.

She slid the shaker along until he could reach it, snatching her hand back as if afraid he might touch her.

"Nice town," he said easily. Maybe her father would have some suggestions for work.

She shrugged, but remained silent, eating, ignoring everyone around her.

His interest piqued, he persisted. He wasn't much with the ladies, too distrustful after the legacy of his mother. But suddenly he wanted to see how far he could push this little thing. Could he get her to talk? Or had she been warned not to talk to strangers?

Normally he was one to let things slide. Not this time; something was goading him. "You live around here long?"

She eyed him suspiciously as she reached for her cup. "All my life," she said.

Hawk froze, fork halfway to his mouth. Her voice sounded like some sultry country singer, low, husky and infinitely sexy. Instant pictures of her murmuring in the dark among the tangle of damp sheets exploded in his mind. The image brought him to full alert. He wanted to hear more.

"In town or on a ranch? From your clothes, you look like you live on a ranch."

"I do."

Not chatty, eh? It was almost more effort than it was worth, just to have someone to talk to while eating.

"Maybe you can help me—" Hawk started.

Just then a rough-looking cowboy stomped across the room on his way out. He paused by the woman and yanked her braid a couple of times. She whirled and knocked his hand away.

"Bug off, Brent," she said, her voice low and angry, her eyes flashing.

"Hey, sweet cakes, what about you going out with me on Saturday night? We can go to the Round-up, drink a few beers, dance a few numbers, then go back to my place. I'll get you home in time for chores the next morning." His leer was so blatant, Hawk was startled. Then the familiar white-hot anger flashed. Instantly he wanted to wipe that lecherous look off the cowboy's face, plant a fist in the center of his gut and wipe the floor with him.

"Go away, I'm not interested." She turned back to her breakfast.

"Come on, sweet cakes, you put out for others, why not me?" The big man almost whined; his hand dropped to her shoulder.

She tried to shrug him off. Hawk noticed the rosy glow of embarrassment in her cheeks. She stared at her plate as if it were the Holy Grail as she tried to ignore the obnoxious man.

Blinding heat surged through Hawk and, without

thinking, he swiveled on his stool, stood and faced the other man, the anger barely controlled. He had to look down; this Brent character was at least four inches shorter.

"The lady told you to leave. I'd suggest you do it right now." His voice was low and mean. Clenching his fists, anger overrode the pain in his bruised hands. The last thing he wanted right now was another fight, but if this bully pushed much more, he'd wade right in.

For a long moment, silence held the diner. No one spoke or moved, all eyes focused on Hawk and Brent. For a second, Hawk saw answering anger flare in the man's eyes, but he backed down. Glancing to the woman then back to Hawk, he smirked. "That's the way of it, eh? Not my turn yet." Holding his hands away from his body, palms up, he stepped around Hawk and headed out the door.

Hawk swept his angry eyes around the rest of the diner. The customers who were staring immediately glanced away. In only seconds the noise resumed a comfortable level. Slowly the anger began to seep away.

"Thank you, but it wasn't necessary to come to my defense. I can handle things." She darted a quick defiant look at Hawk.

"I don't approve of men harassing women." Especially men old enough to know better.

Hawk took a gulp of the coffee, the adrenaline beginning to wane. Hadn't he vowed just minutes before that he was going to learn control?

"I'm Amanda Williams," she said softly.

He looked up. "Hawk Blackstone."

Amanda really looked at the man beside her for the

first time. She had thought his attempts at conversation a subtle pickup, a different tactic from the others she was used to. Maybe she'd been mistaken. His left eye was bruised, his jaw swollen and he needed a shave. He stood tall, broad in the shoulders. The muscles that bulged beneath his cotton shirt gave evidence he was not a stranger to hard work. His clothes were typical of all the men she knew, which proved he was just another randy cowboy. She'd observed his hands earlier. Clearly he'd been in a fight recently. That made it all the more touching that he had been willing to stand up for her against Brent Marshal. It wouldn't have been easy starting out with aches and pains from an earlier fight.

Her heart lurched and raced in her chest. No one had stood up for her before. She was intrigued that a stranger would be willing to do so. Intrigued, and touched, and perplexed.

Obviously he didn't know who she was, or he wouldn't have bothered. Still, the warm glow in her heart did not fade. She relished the cherished feeling that flooded her, caused by a stranger she would probably never see again.

She sighed and turned back to the last of her omelet. He wanted to talk, but she wanted to get out as soon as she could. She shouldn't have come into town for breakfast. The scene was her own fault. She could have eaten at home. But it had been weeks since she had any kind of break and she had wanted to treat herself to a meal that she hadn't fixed. Most of the time if she left the ranch it was to go to Thermopolis, more than thirty miles away. Not to Tagget. There were never any problems in Thermopolis. But in Tagget the possibility always lurked. The worst was never knowing from where it would come. She'd eaten here before without being hassled. But then it had been for lunch and the cowboys weren't present in such number. Brent's rude invitation was probably his way of showing off.

She sighed, drank the last of her coffee and took her bill. With another brief nod to the stranger, she headed for the cash register. She had work to do. No time to worry about Brent and his crude remarks. She should be used to it by now. Nothing had changed in six years, so why did she keep hoping?

Climbing into her pickup truck, Amanda glanced through the diner window and stared at Hawk Blackstone. For a split second something touched her heart. Wondering who he was and if she'd see him again, she started the engine and backed away. It might have been nice to chat casually with him for just a few minutes. She hadn't met anyone new in ages. And, except for Pepe and Walt, she rarely talked to other adults.

Amanda headed for the lumberyard. She needed more fence posts. Riding the perimeter the past few weeks, she had noted the number of posts that needed replacing, most in the draw near Tom Standish's place. She'd pick up some new wire, too.

Before she left town she needed to stop at the feed store to get some supplements for the mare in foal. She hoped Brent was the worst she would face this morning. She didn't relish having to drive to Thermopolis just for the mare's supplements. She would be glad to get back home, where she felt safe.

Maybe she should give up and sell the place. Could she start over somewhere else? Somewhere where no one knew her?

But why should she? She had done nothing wrong. This was her home.

It was the same old argument. And not one she would resolve today. The Royal Flush Ranch belonged to her. She owned it lock, stock and barrel and she wasn't giving it up because of Bobby Jack Pembroke or all his lying friends, or even give in to Robert Pembroke Senior's harassment.

Thirty minutes later Amanda pulled up before the feed store and took a deep breath. She reached for the card she'd written her ad on. Every time she or one of the men came to town, the job offer was listed on the community bulletin board in the feed store. She suspected the owner took it down before she reached home. But maybe one day he'd get tired and leave it up long enough for someone to respond. She badly needed the help.

Entering the open barn of a building, she headed for the large corkboard to the left of the wide double doors. Hawk Blackstone stood before it, reading the cards posted. Hesitating only a moment, Amanda squared her shoulders and walked over.

"Hi again," she said more calmly than she felt. Sitting at the counter, she hadn't realized how tall he was. Nor could her eyes resist skimming over him. She remembered the strong jaw, still in need of a shave. His blue eyes sparkled as he looked down at her, and his slow smile caused her heart to turn somersaults. His jaw was swollen, giving his smile a lopsided look.

"Hello." He touched the rim of his hat with two fingers.

His drawl sent shivers up her spine. Standing as tongue-tied as a young girl, Amanda concentrated on breathing. It was difficult. Warmth crept through her as his eyes roamed across her body, returned to lock with hers. The warmth was unexpected. What was not a surprise was the way he looked at her.

"I was right about the boots," Hawk said.

"Huh?" She had expected something else.

"In the diner I couldn't see what you had on your feet, but I figured boots. Once I heard you lived on a ranch, I knew. But it's nice to have it confirmed." He looked pleased with himself.

She nodded, stepping around him to pull off a thumbtack and pin her notice on the board. As much as she might wish to start a conversation, she had nothing to say. The card posted, Amanda nodded and turned back toward the shelves that held the feed supplements. She needed to buy what she wanted and get back to the ranch. She'd been gone long enough. There was no reason to tarry, and danger of more problems if she did.

Taking two boxes, Amanda walked toward the back. Joe Stevens owned the store. He was talking with two men from the Bar M Bar. Her heart sank. She didn't need this. She was only in town to get supplies, take a short break from the demands of her ranch. Getting hassled twice in one morning was just too much.

For a long heartbeat she considered putting the supplements back on the shelf and sending Walt in to pick them up. But that was foolish. She couldn't spare the time. Tilting her chin determinedly, she marched back to the counter and put the boxes down. Reaching in her pocket for money, she avoided the looks of the two cowhands.

"Well, well. Lookee who's here," Rolly Owens

said, nudging his partner. "Must be our lucky day, Jim."

"Yeah. Getting tired of all those old men yet, darlin'?" Jim asked, throwing his arm across her shoulders.

Amanda stepped away and shrugged him off. Glaring at Jim she spoke coldly, "Keep your hands to yourself." Ignoring them as best she could, she gazed at Joe, angered at his standing by silently. Why didn't he tell those yahoos to leave?

"That'll be $54.86. Cash," Joe said slowly, his eyes insolently running over her.

"Of course." Everyone else in town ran a tab as long as her arm, but not Amanda Williams. For her it was cash the whole way. She should have gone to Thermopolis. Why was she giving her business to this man? Drawing out the crumpled bills and counting the money, she slapped them on the counter. Turning to leave, she stopped, her heart beating heavily. Both cowboys stood between her and the door. Their poses left no doubt what she'd have to put up with to get away. She tilted her chin. Tired as she was of innuendos, she knew better than to let her emotions show.

"Going somewhere, doll?" Jim asked, tilting back his hat and smirking down at her.

"Naw, Jim, she doesn't want to leave before the fun starts, do you, babe?"

"Excuse me, but you're in my way." Hawk came silently up behind the two men and stood legs braced, arms held loose, fingers flexing and fisting. What was it with the men in this town? Did they treat all women like tramps? Or just this one? And why? As far as he could tell she had done nothing to invite this kind of attention.

"This is a private party, mister—stay out," Rolly growled, flicking Hawk a dismissing glance, turning back to Amanda.

"I want to talk to the lady. She's offering a job and I need one."

With that, the two men turned and stared at him. As did Joe. As did Amanda. No one said a word.

Hawk raised the card she had just placed on the bulletin board. "I'd like to apply."

"If you need work, try the Bar M Bar. It's the biggest place around," Jim said, slanting a glance down at Amanda. "You don't want to take the job at the Royal."

Hawk picked up the nuance in his comment. He was being warned off.

"That's for me to decide," he said easily, but shifted just a bit to plant his feet firmly on the warped floorboards. The tension grew as the two cowboys flicked a glance between them as if deciding whether to say more.

Amanda took advantage of the situation and pushed between her tormentors until she stood before Hawk Blackstone. "I need an all-round cowboy. I've got horses and cattle to see to and a whole lot of fencing that needs to be repaired. There's haying in the fall and water holes to keep clear, sick animals to care for and branding and castrating in the spring and fall."

"I've been on ranches since I was a tot. I can do anything you need doing. And get it done faster and better than anyone else you know."

She almost smiled at his bragging, but something held her back. Looking at his quiet confidence, she suddenly realized he probably could do just that. She took a deep breath. His scent filled her nostrils, enticing and disturbing. Shocked, she could not move. She didn't need some sort of attraction for the man. For heaven's sake, look where her last case of attraction got her.

But she was desperate for help and he was the first to respond to her ad in the year she'd been posting it. How dangerous could it be to hire him? He'd stay in the bunkhouse with Walt and Pepe. She had enough chores for him to do that he'd be too tired to try anything even if he wanted to. And he'd been nothing but polite with her, so why did she even consider that he might try something?

Would that change?

"When could you start?" she asked, ignoring the tendrils of excitement that shimmered along her nerve endings. She needed a hand, he was applying, that was all there was to it.

"Right now." He reached out and took the boxes of feed supplements from her hands and turned toward the wide open door. "My gear is at the bus depot. I've got a list of ranches you can call to verify my background."

"Don't do it, mister. There'll be hell to pay if you do," Rolly warned.

Hawk glanced at the man, narrowing his eyes at the deliberate threat. "Now, or later?" The answer came low, soft and clear. He was not going to be intimidated by some two-bit cowboy throwing his weight around.

The man glanced at his friend, then looked away.

"I'll be waiting," Hawk taunted. He touched his

finger to the brim of his hat and turned with Amanda and headed out.

"You came in on the bus?" she asked, pausing by the old pickup she drove.

"Yes. This morning." He paused and looked down the main street of Tagget. It looked like all the other ranch towns he'd lived in. Some of the buildings were old with the false wooden fronts of typical Western towns. A couple looked new, more glass than anything. The street was clean, the few cars out this early parked nose into the sidewalks.

Time he found a place for himself and stayed. He glanced at the woman studying him and grinned. "Need to clean up a bit, I reckon."

She glanced again at his chin. No wonder he needed a shave. He'd probably been on the bus all night. "We'll get your gear and head for the ranch."

In less than ten minutes they were on the road that led from Tagget to the Royal Flush Ranch. The Wind River range rose on their left, the spring grass still belly deep against the cattle that grazed in its lushness. The sky was a clear blue, the forecast for a warm day.

The truck ate up the miles. As she competently drove, Hawk watched the passing scenery, with only an occasional glance at his driver, more curious about her than he'd ever been about other women he'd met casually. Primary in his mind was the question of how old she was.

"You authorized to hire for the ranch?" he asked lazily.

She flicked him a quick look and nodded. "It's my ranch, I reckon I can hire anyone I want."

She noticed he looked startled. What was wrong

with a woman owning a ranch? She could run it as well as any man. Almost, anyway. If she could get competent help, she had the potential to own a showplace. And make money to boot.

"Want to tell me what was going on with those men back in town?"

She shrugged. That was not something she wanted to discuss. She knew he'd find out sooner or later. What would happen then? Would he come on to her like the men in town, or would he haul leather and clear out before she could get any work done?

She'd soon find out.

Cocking a sassy grin at him, she took a deep breath. "Haven't you figured it out by now, cowboy? I'm the town bad girl."

"Right, pull the other one," he replied, chuckling softly.

Amanda blinked. It was hardly the reaction she'd expected. "You don't think so?" she asked, perplexed. Everyone in Tagget knew her reputation. No one had doubted Bobby Jack's word for an instant. Nor all his friends. No one had believed her. Yet this stranger apparently wasn't buying into it.

"Sugar, you are too young and too innocent to ever play that role. Your behavior with those testosterone-laden cowboys back there was the exact opposite of the actions of any bad girl I ever knew. And, sugar, I've known plenty in my time."

She could believe that. It took a bad boy to really know bad girls, and she would bet he was a champ. Even with the bruises and day-old beard, he was a heart-stopper. His blue eyes matched the cloudless Wyoming sky, clear and true. Yet they could freeze up instantly, or flame to lethal intensity as they had when facing down first Brent, then Rolly and Jim.

His casual sprawled posture in the truck enticed her. She had never been so aware of another person in her life. Especially a man. She felt crowded by him, yet he had not crossed the center line. His long legs were cramped; she had the seat too far forward for him to be comfortable. Yet he'd never said a word.

"Don't call me sugar. You don't know me and we certainly aren't close enough for endearments," she snapped. Was he going to display typical male arrogance? Had she made a mistake hiring him?

His glance heated her skin. She shivered slightly and frowned. She had no business feeling anything for this stranger. If he could do a day's work, he'd help her out. If not, she'd fire him. That was all that was between them—business. She would not let his gaze start butterflies dancing in her stomach. She would not let his grin melt her bones. She would not let his mere presence start dreams that had lain dormant for more than half a decade. She would not—

She would not be able to work with him for ten minutes without making a blathering idiot of herself if she didn't garner some self-control. So he was a woman's dream. He was still a man, and she knew better than to trust any man under the age of sixty.

Two

Hawk continued to study Amanda as she drove, wondering why she'd made such a statement. She was like no bad girl he'd ever met. He'd glimpsed a hint of vulnerability beneath her bravado front. She had tried to brush it off, for that he gave her credit. But if it were true, it would have to hurt. She was too innocent to relish a label like that one. Where had it come from? At least that explained the insulting behavior of the men in Tagget. But were the men blind?

For one surprising moment he felt a surge of protective anger for the young woman sitting beside him. He looked away, questioning it. He had not looked after anyone in his life. Where did this protective urge come from? Hell, he had to get his own life in order; he didn't have time to delve in anyone else's problems. She could take care of herself. She'd held her own with Brent in the café. If he hadn't stepped in at the feed store, he knew she would probably have managed the two rowdy cowboys.

Yet he had a strong urge to return to town and teach them all some manners. Make sure they knew to leave her alone on her next visit, or answer to him.

He shook his head again. He had no business thinking like that. He planned to work temporarily while he put out feelers to purchase his own ranch. He knew what he wanted: a flourishing spread in Montana or Wyoming. He wanted to try some crossbreeding, see what kind of results he could get with a program designed to produce heavy meat on each steer, crossed with leaner cuts.

The truck slowed and turned onto a rutted driveway. Amanda slowed down for the familiar cattle grid and immediately her heart lightened. This place belonged to her, thanks to old Jonas Harper. It could never be taken from her. She would hold on to it so she could pass it on to Joey. The pain from the confrontations in town faded as she lovingly gazed across the range.

"Welcome to Royal Flush Ranch," she said proudly, the thrill of ownership still catching her unaware.

"Unusual name," Hawk commented, his eyes curious as he studied the spread. The grass grew high, the fencing along the dirt track stretched out intact. In the distance he saw a small herd of horses.

"That part of your herd?" he asked, nodding in their direction.

"Yes. Quarter horses. I love horses, have been expanding that herd for the past five years. Last year I had my first sale. I did well." Pride and satisfaction resounded in her statement. She had accomplished that on her own. It hadn't mattered she had had to drive all the way to Cheyenne to get a good price, she'd done it. Jonas had scoffed at her ideas, yet still let her try them out. For a moment sadness touched her. She wished he had lived to see the success of that first sale.

She wished he had lived long enough for her to have thanked him for saving her life, for offering her a home and refuge. She hoped he had known how grateful she'd always been.

"You run cattle, as well?"

"Yes. The main cash crop is cattle. The horses were just something I wanted to do. Jonas indulged me."

"Diversification."

"Fun." She flicked a gamine grin and shrugged. "The nice part is making a bit of money on the side." Money she had needed to keep the place going. Cash money to keep things afloat when she couldn't get a loan. Money she had not put into Robert Pembroke's bank.

"How did the ranch get its name?"

"Jonas's grandfather won it in a poker game in the first part of the century, with a royal flush. He changed the name. Most folks just call it the Royal." It had been in Jonas's family more than eighty years. Now it was hers.

Hawk slowly rubbed his fingers against his bruised jaw. "Who's Jonas?"

She remained silent for a moment, guiding the truck over the uneven roadway. One day she wanted enough cash to have the road graded. "Jonas Harper. He owned this place. He died last year."

"Your father?"

"No. He was the man I lived with." She almost held her breath. She could have explained, but didn't bother. No one else had cared, why would a stranger? And she was not ashamed of her relationship with Jonas. He had offered her a home when her own mother had turned her out. She would never forget that! And because of that, she ignored the talk in town. Avoided going into town for the most part.

The man she lived with. He should have expected it. She was too pretty to live alone. How old was she? If she'd lived here for a while she had to be older than she appeared. Her skin looked as soft as a rose petal. He wanted to brush his rough fingers down it to test its softness. She wore no makeup, but her coloring didn't require any. The sooty lashes that framed her eyes were dark enough. Her lips were faintly pink and looked warm and inviting. He stifled a groan and looked away. Fantasizing about kissing his new boss would definitely not insure he keep the job. And he sure as hell didn't like the tingle of jealousy that hovered since he'd heard about Jonas. He had just met the woman, what she had done with her life before was none of his business. What she did in the future was none of his business, either.

She was his boss, nothing more. And only as long as it took him to find a place of his own.

Amanda pulled up before an old frame house. She cut the engine and stared at it, seeing it as Hawk would see it. The paint had long faded and peeled. The trim was warped and worn. The roof had more patches than a patchwork quilt. It needed work. Yet it was home. And it was hers.

"Mommy, Mommy, you're home!" The screen

door slammed as a small bundle of energy flew out and raced down the stairs to the truck.

Hawk felt as if he'd been kicked. *Amanda was a mother!*

She opened the door and hopped out, scooping up the little boy and hugging him as she twirled the two of them around in the dirt yard.

"Yes, I'm back. Were you a good boy?" She tightened her hold for a moment, then brushed her lips across his cheek and set him down. He still put up with mushy stuff, as he called it, as long as she didn't indulge too much.

"Yes, I was. I did all the chores Walt wanted me to do and I ate all my breakfast. Did you have breakfast in town? Did you have pancakes?"

She ruffled his hair and shook her head. "No, I had an omelet. It was delicious, though."

"I wanted to go." His bottom lip stuck out.

"Maybe next time," she hedged. She would not take him into town. She would not expose her precious baby to the chance of malicious tongues. Things were hard enough without that.

Hawk closed the passenger door and reached into the back of the pickup truck for his duffel. He slung his saddle across his shoulder and turned toward the barn, stifling a curse at the pull against his ribs.

"Wait, I'll show you the way," Amanda called.

He turned back to look at her and her son. He said nothing, just waited. She scooted around the truck, her hand still holding the boy's. Was he Jonas's boy? *The man I lived with.* Why hadn't Jonas married her, especially if there was a child?

"I figure the saddle can go in the barn. The bunkhouse can't be far." His stride long, he did nothing to shorten it. If she wanted to keep up with him, she had to hurry.

"No horse?" she asked, eyeing the fancy saddle.

"I ride the ranch's horses."

"But don't use the ranch tack?" She had to walk fast to keep up with him; Joey almost ran.

"Won it in a rodeo. It suits me."

"Hawk, stop a minute. I want you to meet my son."

He stopped and turned, looking down at the small boy. He was a cute kid with hair almost the same color as his mother, his eyes wide and expressive and a deep, dark brown. Shyly the boy gazed up at him. For once Hawk was at a loss for words. He didn't know what to say to a kid.

"Hawk Blackstone, this is Joey Williams. Joey, Hawk is going to work for us."

"Like Walt and Pepe?" he asked, his eyes never leaving Hawk.

"Yes."

"Hi," Joey said shyly, grinning.

Hawk stared. The kid didn't resemble Amanda much, but he had the same gamine grin his mother had. He looked at Amanda, and his temperature rose a notch. She stared back at him, her lips parted slightly as if breathing hard. When her tongue darted out to lick her lower lip, he almost lost it. Taking a deep breath, he turned and stomped toward the barn. He needed to get to work. Work hard, sleep hard—alone. For a split second he pictured himself sleeping with his new boss, her chestnut hair spread around a pillow, her gray eyes wide and luminous with desire. His fingers tracing over that soft skin that looked so much like rose petals. *Damn!*

Shivering sensations swept through her. Amanda watched Hawk walk away and wondered if her knees would hold her up. His look had been as potent as a torch. When he'd gazed at her mouth, she felt as if a spear of heat had shafted her. She couldn't believe she'd touched her tongue to her lips, as if enticing him. She'd read enough romance novels to know behavior like that told a man that a woman was interested. Did he suspect her of flirting?

But she wasn't. She just been startled at her reaction to his look. It had never happened to her before. Not even with Bobby Jack. Hawk touched something very basic within her and she didn't have any idea of how to stop it. So her eyes followed him as he moved away. He walked with an arrogant damn-your-eyes strut that was pure male. His long legs ate up the distance. Even beneath the weight of the saddle and the duffel, he moved as easily as any predatory male. A wolf on the prowl, a cougar on the hunt. She shivered, but not with fear. A tantalizing anticipation bubbled up. Mesmerized, she started after him.

"Come on, Joey, we'll show Hawk the bunkhouse."

"He's awfully big, Mommy," Joey said as they walked toward the barn.

"Yes, but he would never hurt you." Did her son fear the cowboy?

"I know. He's just big, like a giant. Walt and Pepe aren't so big anymore."

She smiled. For most of his life, Joey had known few men; Jonas, Walt, Pepe and Mike Peters, the local vet. None were imposing men. Not like Hawk. Maybe broadening her son's exposure to another man would be good.

Dumping his saddle across an open stall door, Hawk lowered his duffel and surveyed the barn. It was in better shape than her house. The loft still contained a few bales of last year's hay, the sweet aroma mingled with that of dirt and heat and horses. The stalls were empty, their doors standing wide. He glanced into the one nearest him. Filled with clean straw, it was in good repair. Beyond, a second half door opened to the corral. A dozen horses dozed in the sun.

He turned. She stood in the center of the barn, the light behind her. Her silhouette was dainty, feminine despite the jeans and cotton shirt. Her breasts filled the shirt, which then narrowed at her waist. Her hips flared gently out, and he felt an unexpected and strong pull of sexual attraction. Gritting his teeth, he clamped down on it. It had been a while since he'd had a woman, but he wasn't traveling down that road anytime soon. And especially not with his new boss. He needed his energies focused on getting a ranch of his own. Now that he'd made the decision, he wanted to implement it as soon as possible. He'd stay to help around the Royal until he found the place he wanted. Then he'd be gone. And he wasn't going to tangle with any woman in the meantime. Especially one with a kid.

"The bunkhouse is around to the side," Amanda said.

"I could have found it."

He could do anything he set his mind to, she thought hours later as she stirred the thick rich stew that bubbled on the stove. He'd stowed his things and presented himself for work. Walt had quickly listed a number of chores that Hawk could do. When Walt had stopped by a little while ago, he couldn't sing praises high enough for the man. All the tasks were completed. To a man of Walt's years, the chores would have taken far longer and tired him out. Hawk was still raring to go.

The man radiated energy. She had lived with old men too long. She was used to a slower pace. Maybe one new, young cowboy was all she needed. Maybe between the four of them they could keep up with the myriad tasks that constantly needed doing on a working ranch.

In the meantime, she'd caught up on the paperwork that had piled up, unloaded the truck and drawn up a schedule of chores for the men to do over the next few days. Normally one to pitch in and help right along with Walt and Pepe, she made sure she had her fair share of tasks. But none that would take her near Hawk.

She couldn't supervise him. He had probably forgotten more about ranching than she had learned. But that wasn't the reason. Her reactions around him scared her. She didn't want to give the impression she'd be interested in anything more than a strictly business relationship.

Yet when the men came in for dinner, her eyes immediately sought him. The kitchen was big, but once he entered, the room seemed to shrink. He had showered and shaved. His bruises showed even stronger, but it wasn't his bruises she stared at. He glanced over to her and gave that slow one-sided grin that caused her heart to trip faster and faster. Heat rose in her cheeks, and she turned swiftly, lest the telltale color give away her thoughts.

Joey watched Hawk with big eyes, clearly fascinated by the man. He asked questions incessantly until Amanda stopped him. "Eat up. Hawk will be here
long enough to answer your questions over the next
few days. You don't have to ask everything tonight."

"Are you staying forever?" Joey asked one more.

Before Hawk could reply, Amanda shook her head.
"No, Hawk doesn't stay long in any place." Her eyes
met his, challenging. He'd given her the list of places
he had worked and she had called every one. All had
the same thing to say: he proved to be an excellent
cowboy, but he had a temper to match the devil's.
When he got riled, he got out of control. He'd been
fired for fighting at four of the places she'd called.

Hawk's eyes held hers, his expression tight and
tinged with anger. Surely he had expected her to call,
otherwise why would he have given her the list?

"Your mother's right, Joey," he said, his gaze
locked with Amanda's. "I don't stay long in any one
place. I'll stay for a while, then be moving on." He
glanced around. "I'm looking to buy a spread of my
own. I have a real estate agent working it. If something gets put on the market that's suitable, I'll take
it."

How long would that take? she longed to ask. *Long
enough for me to grow to depend on you? To have
this attraction develop into something more?*

Dragging her eyes away, Amanda turned to ask
Walt how his day had gone. Walt Johnson and Pepe
Gonzales had both worked for Jonas. Both men were
in their late sixties. While Walt was slowing down
and even admitted to problems with arthritis, Pepe
was still as wiry and strong as he had been as a young

man. His only concession to age was the gradual loss of hearing.

"I checked on the fencing at the draw. It's down," Walt said.

Amanda sighed, looking at her stew. It was enough to drive away her appetite. "Damn. Though I expected it. I bought extra fence posts."

"We'll need them. They chopped up four this time."

"What are you talking about?" Hawk asked, intrigued by the conversation.

The three adults looked at one another. Then Walt spoke. "We have a problem with one of our neighbors. Somehow the fence between our property keeps being cut and—"

"Tom Standish and his men cut it, you mean," Amanda interrupted.

"We don't know that for sure."

"I do."

"Why would he do something like that?" Hawk asked.

"General harassment," she snapped.

"Who's general harassment?" Joey asked, his eyes bright with interest.

"Just a dumb old man who couldn't lead an army. Have you finished? You can take a brownie outside if you want." She didn't want to discuss this in front of Joey. The longer she could keep him sheltered from the harshness of life, the better for him. He was only a baby, just five. Time enough for him to find out how unfair life could be when he was older.

The others took her cue and remained silent until the little boy had disappeared and the screen door slammed shut.

"What's going on?" Hawk asked, his gaze hard and direct.

"Tom Standish wants to buy the ranch. He's offered several times since Jonas died. I don't want to sell. So this is his way of driving me nuts."

"He cuts the fence, drives his cattle on our range, then calls up and complains," Pepe added.

"Tell the sheriff," Hawk suggested.

Amanda gave a mirthless laugh. "Right. He wants to help me as much as he wants to lose the next election. I don't have any proof, according to Sheriff Yates, so his hands are tied."

"So where does that leave us?" Hawk asked.

She stared. *Us?*

Slowly he smiled at her look. "I ride for the brand. That makes it us."

He almost laughed at her look of pure astonishment. Hadn't anyone ever been on her side? Except for these two old men, of course. She intrigued him more than the situation with her neighbor. Who was Amanda Williams? And what would it take to gain her trust?

"Well, if you have any ideas on stopping Tom, do let the rest of us know," she snapped.

"Maybe. Tomorrow you and I will take a ride out and you can show me the place."

"If you could stop old Tom, you'd be a hero, son," Pepe said.

A hero. Hawk shook his head. The last thing he'd ever be was a hero. But he wondered if he could make a difference to Amanda. If he could stop the hassles from her neighbors, would the woman be a little grateful? Grateful enough for a kiss? A real one. Not some little peck on the cheek, but a full-blown, tongue-twining, hot-bodies-touching kiss?

He dropped his gaze to the beef stew and filled his fork. He was getting plumb loco, and no better than the locals if he let his thoughts drift along those lines. But he could tell himself whatever he wanted, his body wouldn't listen. He wanted her.

God, he was losing it. A woman he'd met for the first time at breakfast and already he wanted her more than he'd ever wanted another woman? He'd had his share of rodeo groupies flocking around a man, proposing all kinds of celebratory offerings. He'd taken a few up on their suggestions. But it had meant nothing, just the release from the tension of the events.

This was different. He wanted to find out what made her tick, what her secrets were, *how old she was.* She had a son, so she couldn't be as young as she looked. But he still didn't know that very basic fact.

"How old are you?" Hawk asked abruptly.

Amanda stared at him in astonishment. Where had that question come from? What prompted it? Pepe coughed and picked up his glass, hiding his smile behind it. Walt looked back and forth between the two of them.

"I'm twenty-three. How old are you?"

Relief hit him in the chest. She was more than old enough to vote. "Turned thirty day before yesterday," he replied. "How old is Joey?" He might as well get everything straight while he was making a fool of himself. He threw a hot glare at Pepe, but the older man refused to meet his eyes. Pepe's gaze fixed on the table midway between Hawk and Amanda. He looked as if he were probably about to bust a gut laughing.

"He'll be six in a few weeks." She waited. It wouldn't take a rocket scientist to figure out how old she'd been when Joey was born. Now what would he say?

"Thought you were younger. You look it." Damn, she'd been a kid herself when the boy had been born. Even more reason for that Jonas to marry her. What had the man been thinking about?

Conversation came to a ragged stop. The men ate silently. Amanda toyed with her food. She'd nibbled as she cooked. It was a good thing, because her appetite had fled. She wanted to explain so Hawk understood things weren't as bad as they appeared. She needed him to stay, wanted to get Hawk's assurance that he'd stay long enough to help her out. Yet he was a stranger. One who never stayed anywhere very long, according to the various ranch managers he'd worked for.

"Mighty fine eating, Amanda." Walt clattered his fork down on his empty plate and smiled at her.

She smiled and thanked him. He said the same thing every night when he finished eating. It was nice that there were some things that could be counted on.

"I have brownies for dessert." Using the excuse, she shoved back her chair and began to clear her plate and his. Pepe pushed his empty plate over.

"I'll take my brownie back to the bunkhouse. There's a show I want to see."

"You talking about that one on the NASCAR races?" Walt asked.

At Pepe's nod, Walt asked to take dessert with him, as well.

In only seconds Hawk and Amanda were alone.

Her heart skipped a beat when she looked at him and found his blazing blue eyes on her. ''There's more stew, want some?'' Good grief, was that crack in her voice from nerves? She had been standing up to men for years, what was with this stranger?

''I'll take another plateful. And another biscuit if there are any. You always cook for the crew?''

She nodded. When she'd filled his plate, she turned to the sink and slowly began washing up. If she could draw it out until he finished, he'd leave for the bunkhouse and she'd find some breathing room.

''Tell me more about this situation with your neighbor,'' Hawk asked. The food was good and filling. Her biscuits were as light as air. And the lady was as nervous as a mare in heat. Did he make her so?

He carried his plate to the sink where she stood up to her elbows in suds. Sliding it into the warm water, he leaned against the counter, so close he could count the handful of freckles across her nose, see the peeling skin from sunburn.

''Your neighbor,'' he prompted.

''Tom Standish. When Jonas died, he decided he wanted the land. He offered me a ridiculously low amount. I refused. After that it seems like every time I turn around he's cut the fence, pushed his cattle on my range or complained that I have cattle on his.''

''Seems to me he would have done better to court Jonas's widow than try to harass her,'' Hawk said. He was testing the waters. Maybe he'd been mistaken about Jonas and Amanda.

Amanda looked up at that, her gaze meeting his.

"I wasn't married to Jonas, if that's what you're fishing for."

"Sorry, thought you might have been for him to have left you the ranch."

"I think I was the person most surprised to find he'd left me the ranch. I always thought he'd leave it to Walt. They were boyhood friends."

Boyhood friends? Walt had to be close to seventy! "How old was Jonas?"

"Sixty-seven when he died last year," she said. His face registered his surprise. She reached blindly for the last plate and rinsed it off. He deserved to know the whole story, but she hated to tell it.

His hand came under her chin and forced her face around until it tilted toward his. He leaned over and stared deep into her gray eyes. "Tell me about living with Jonas. He was almost fifty years older than you."

Heat stained her cheeks. "I didn't live with him like that, even though people in town insist on thinking so. He offered me a place to stay and a job when…when I needed one badly. I was the cook. I've done the cooking for everyone since I came here. He taught me more and more about ranching over the years and now I do more than just cook, but every day I still make the meals."

"How big is this place?"

"Thirty-two thousand acres of deeded land. I lease some from BLM. The Royal runs over sixty thousand acres all told." The warmth from his hand traveled through her. His calluses were hard against the soft skin covering her jaw, but she didn't care. It was the first time a man had touched her in a long time. He

could hold her from now until dawn if he wanted.
She just wished—

"For sixty thousand acres, you don't have much
help."

"I've been trying to hire men since before Jonas
died. You're the first to respond to my ad."

"And why is that?"

She licked her lips and shook her head. "I've
stopped taking ads in the paper because of the ex-
pense." And the fact the ads always had something
wrong, either the phone number or the salary amount.
"Joe takes down my postings at the feed store almost
as soon as I put them up. And you have to admit
Tagget, Wyoming, is not the hot spot of the world.
We don't have a lot of transients passing through.
Most of the cowboys around here already work at the
other ranches."

"You'd better clear the whole situation up for me,
sugar, just so I know where we stand. Start with the
behavior of the men in town and end with what you
plan to do to stop your neighbor from ripping up your
fences." His breath skimmed across her cheeks, his
thumb moved slightly against her heated skin.

Swallowing hard, Amanda knew she had to move
before she did something foolish like respond to his
touch. She reached for his wrist, her soapy fingers
slipping against his taut skin as she tried to grab on
and pull him away. Without effort he resisted. His
touch remained gentle, but his arm felt like granite.

"Things weren't so bad before Jonas died. He did
most of the trips to town. He or Walt. And we had
four more men until the past couple of years. Then
for different reasons they left. I used to stay at the
house and take care of the meals and the paperwork,

but when we became shorthanded, I started helping with the cattle and my horses. I started homeschooling for Joey, too. When Jonas died, things changed.'' This was so hard. She hated it. ''I had to start going to town. And you must know small towns, you've lived in plenty. Gossip is like its life blood. I had a bellyful when I was younger, thanks to Bobby Jack. It started up again, only this time rumors flew about me and Jonas.''

''Who's Bobby Jack?''

''He's Joey's father.'' She held her breath, waiting for the condemnation.

At that, Hawk released her and stepped back. He ran his fingers through his dark hair and blew out a deep breath. Leaning against the counter, he stared at the toe of his boots, trying to take it all in.

''It's a bit complicated,'' she offered tentatively, wiping her wet hands on the seat of her jeans.

''All tied up with being the town bad girl, I suppose.'' He deliberately kept his tone neutral. Maybe he'd misjudged the woman. Maybe she was capable of—

''That's a reputation I don't deserve! I avoid Tagget as much as possible because I was labeled with that tag years ago and no one lets go.'' Her voice rang strong, assured, her stance bracing. Her hands on her hips, she faced him, as if daring him to challenge her.

''Back down, sugar. I'm not your enemy. You're right—it sounds complicated. So let's take the brownies outside and sit on that porch swing I saw. You can tell me in words of one syllable so I can understand,'' Hawk said easily.

''I don't think so. It's really none of your business.

You're here to work on the ranch until you decide to take off again. If you want to leave now, there's the door.'' She kept her anger fanned. She hadn't backed down for the whole town, she wasn't going to start now!

He reached around her and picked up the plate of still-warm brownies. Grabbing her upper arm in one strong hand, he turned her around and marched her through the house.

"Stop it, Hawk. What are you doing?''

"We're going to talk. If I ever saw anyone in need of some help, it's you. And fixing a cut fence isn't the extent of it. But I deserve to know the whole story. You owe me.''

She dug in her heels, temporarily stopping their progression. "I don't owe you anything. Men think just because—''

"I'm not men. I'm just one man, Hawk Blackstone. And you owe me an explanation so I'm as clear as I can be on the players and the play. That way I don't step on the wrong toes.''

"Step on toes?'' She didn't understand. He took advantage of her uncertainty to propel her the rest of the way to the wide front porch. The sun was a fiery ball low on the horizon. The fresh scent of grass and clean fresh air blew in a gentle breeze. In the distance to the left, Joey hung on the corral fence, petting one of the horses.

"Sit.'' He sank on the bench seat of the swing, waited for her to join him, then pushed it back and forth. Offering her a brownie, he settled the plate on his lap and took the largest he could find. He loved brownies. He'd do well to remember who made them if he wanted any more.

"Tell me about Bobby Jack. Where does he live now?"

"He died just before Jonas did, over a year ago. Before that he lived in town. He worked at the bank his father owns."

"Bobby Jack." Hawk said the name as if it was a joke.

"Robert Jackson Pembroke. He was always called Bobby Jack, so people would know it wasn't his father, Robert."

"You two ever marry?"

"Never." The bitterness shone through.

"Why not?"

She jumped up and crossed to the railing, leaning on the crosspiece. She hated the entire situation. Nothing ever changed. Nothing ever got better. "He said Joey wasn't his." He'd said a lot more, but that was the statement that hurt the most. Bobby Jack had known Joey was his, and repudiated his own son. She didn't think she would ever forgive him for that. She could take the dirt he had dished out, but his repudiation had hurt more than anything.

Three

Joey spotted his mother and ran from the corral, a bright grin on his face. Amanda watched her son coming, her heart melting at his darling face. She loved him more than anything. Despite everything that had happened, she would not change a single minute if it meant he turned out any differently.

"I counted the horses, Mommy." He thundered up the wooden steps and paused, breathing hard, by the swing. Hawk smiled and lifted him up to sit beside him.

"So you can count," he murmured, offering the boy a brownie.

"Mommy teached me. I can count to a hundred. Want to hear?"

"Another time, honey. You need to get ready for bed," Amanda said gently, crossing the porch and reaching out to brush his hair from his forehead. "Didn't you already have a brownie?"

"Hawk gave me this one. You don't want to mess with him," Joey said with great certainty.

"Oh, and why is that?" She couldn't help the smile. He looked so solemn sitting by the big dark man.

"He's so big he could break you into little pieces."

"Joey, I would never hurt your mother. She's a lady." Hawk spoke to the boy, but his eyes never left his mother.

Amanda flushed at the implied compliment. Despite what she'd said, he still thought her a lady. No one else had ever treated her so well.

"Come on, buckaroo, time for bed." She looked away, wondering if the weakness in her knees meant she was coming down with the flu.

"I'll wait here," Hawk said.

She had hoped Joey would prove the excuse to avoid any more discussions. She felt restless, unsettled. She didn't like thinking about the past and all the mistakes she'd made. She wished she could wipe the slate clean and start over somewhere far away where no one knew her. But that would mean leaving the ranch, and she didn't want to do that. It was her home, hers and Joey's.

"I could be a while," she said, not wanting to return.

"I'm not going anywhere. I still want more information about your neighbor."

Reluctantly she nodded, then led Joey into the house.

Hawk sat on the swing thinking about what she'd told him. Idly munching brownies, he pushed back

and forth and considered the situation. He didn't like
the implications that the sheriff wouldn't help. His
older brother was a district attorney in Cheyenne.
Both of them had a healthy regard for the law.

He rose and carried the plate back into the kitchen.
He could hear the murmur of voices upstairs. A childish laugh rang out. Hawk cocked his head listening.
How many years since he'd heard a kid laugh? A long
time. He felt the warmth of the old house seep into
his consciousness. He couldn't remember a time when
he had felt so at home. His father had become a bitter
man when his wife left. None of the warmth Amanda
displayed for her son had been forthcoming in his
father's household, even after he married Ellen.

Hawk reached for the phone. He was going to
check in with his brother, ask a couple of questions.
Worrying about a family and home life had no place
in his thoughts. He did not plan to have a family.
When he bought his ranch, his time would be full
enough without the aggravation of others to consider.
Besides, with his father's two wives as examples,
Hawk didn't trust the institution of marriage. Women
didn't stick around. They came, stole your heart, then
trampled it in their haste to depart with all your
worldly goods. It was not for him.

When Amanda came back out onto the porch a half
hour later, Hawk sat in the swing. It was full dark,
the evening stars offering faint light in the inky black
sky. The breeze had died. It was still, quiet, cool.

"Joey asleep?" His voice washed over her, deep,
sexy.

She shivered and nodded. He couldn't see. "Yes,
he's asleep." Slowly she walked to the railing, turned
and propped her bottom on the flat crosspiece. She

looked toward Hawk, but couldn't see him against the darkness of the house.

"You were telling me about Bobby Jack," he offered.

Amanda leaned against the column. She didn't need to tell this cowboy anything. She could just order him to do his job. Yet, telling wouldn't change anything. And maybe he did need a clear picture so he'd continue to ride for the brand. She stared across the yard toward the barn, once again reliving her foolishness.

"Bobby Jack took me out the summer between my junior and senior year in high school. He was already in college. His family was one of the richest in town—his dad owns the bank. I knew who he was most of my life. And had a crush on him from my first day in high school. I thought it a miracle he'd asked me out. Right, some miracle."

The swing squeaked as Hawk stood and stepped nearer.

"So you became a twosome that summer and then he returned to college?"

She swung around, trying to see him in the dim light. "No. Nothing so nice. We had a few dates. Clandestine ones, at that. I thought it was so romantic, he didn't want to share his time with me with others. Ha! That had nothing to do with it." If she had had more experience, if she'd only suspected from the beginning—

"My mother was, um, rather well-known in town for being…friendly when someone took her out. Bobby Jack expected the same thing from me."

And obviously got it, Hawk thought briefly.

"I know what you think. And it doesn't matter,"

she said quickly. "It shouldn't matter." Her voice changed, grew softer. "But for the record, I thought I was in love, I thought he loved me." Silently she remembered that young innocent girl, who had been so happy for three exciting weeks one summer. Then so shattered.

"Date rape?" Hawk said instantly.

She tilted her head, "No, he didn't force me. I thought we were in love."

"But he wasn't." Hawk made it a statement.

She shook her head. "No. He wasn't. Once he got what he wanted, he couldn't get away fast enough. He was one of the few boys I'd gone out with. I was so thrilled when he asked me out. I had saved money from working afternoons at the drugstore and bought a new blouse to wear that night. I'd done my hair and splurged to buy makeup. I didn't have a lot of friends to share my joy with. I had to work to help out at home. But I held the dates to my heart until that night. Pride goes before a fall, right?"

Hawk stepped closer, eased down on the railing beside her. "So what happened?" She was so young now, he had a hard time imagining her much younger. She had been just a child.

"My mother said I should have expected it. To stop whining and make sure he asked me out again. She saw Bobby Jack as my ticket to money. When he didn't ask me out again, she got mad."

"And were you mad?"

"Not then, only incredible hurt. Shortly after school started, I realized I was pregnant. I contacted him and he laughed in my face. Said he'd deny sleeping with me from here to forever, and he had five friends who would swear to everyone they had slept with me. So how could I pinpoint any one of them as the father? Trashy girls get what they deserve, I believe he said.''

She shuddered again as the nightmare replayed itself. She had heard the words over and over through the years. Nothing ever changed them. They were engraved on her heart.

Amanda drew herself up. It was in the past. Bobby Jack was dead now, and nothing would change the naive seventeen-year-old she'd been. She had her life now, and didn't need anybody making a play for her.

Hawk swore. Anger flared at the injustice. For a moment he regretted the man's death. He wanted to drive into town and beat the tar out of him.

"And to make sure I couldn't pin it on him, he had his friends spread their lies around the entire town." She pushed off and stood, meeting Hawk's eyes in the dim light. Her voice hardened, her stance grew defensive. "Suddenly I was considered the local slut. My mother had started seeing a John Deere salesman, and she was furious that I might ruin her chances with him. When the talk in town was most rampant, she threw me out of the house. Jonas took me in. He'd been one of my mother's special friends in the past and had always liked me.''

Thank God for Jonas. She could still remember the fear that afternoon, before Jonas had found her. She had a home, a job and a future, all thanks to Jonas Harper. She'd never forget it.

"Not that this is any of your business, I'm just giving you the background so you'll see what I'm up against. Talk and innuendos are all against me. Bobby Jack's daddy is a big influence in Tagget, so of course his son was to be believed before me. That's why I don't go into town much. That's why the sheriff won't do anything on my accusation—he's friends with Robert Pembroke and Tom Standish. I think they would all like it just fine if I left Tagget and never returned.''

''Well, time to change things.'' Hawk's voice came out a growl. Anger shot through him and he grew frustrated as hell because there was nothing he could do to right the wrong. He hated injustice. Didn't have much tolerance for stupidity, either. But his fists could not solve this mess. If anything was to be done, he had to use his brains. He almost laughed. After years of riding the rodeo circuit and working as a thirty-dollar-a-day man, he was going to try to outsmart a bunch of vindictive men bent on destroying this young woman?

Hell, yes. His father hadn't been too smart in dealing with women, but he'd always been there physically for his son, provided a roof over his head, even if it had come with daily lectures. Joey Williams didn't have that. Maybe it was time he had someone to stand up for his mother.

''Ever try to force Bobby Jack to make support payments?'' he asked.

''You're kidding, right? I couldn't even get my own mother on my side, you think anyone else would have listened to anything I said? The bank holds the mortgage on most places in town. It's the only place in town to get car loans. The Pembrokes wield a lot of power in Tagget.''

''They're only men, sugar.''

''I didn't try,'' she said flatly.

''So Jonas took you in, sheltered you, and when he died the wolves circled.''

She smiled at his analogy. "You could say that."

His fist opened and he turned his hand, grasping her fingers in his, holding her small hand against his palm. He could feel her calluses press against his. Slowly he rubbed his thumb back and forth, relishing the satiny texture of the back of her hand. He knew she must feel like that all over. When she tugged her hand to free it, his grip tightened. He didn't want to let her go.

Amanda's breath caught as Hawk traced his thumb across her wrist. Her body tingled in awakening awareness. She felt brilliantly alive, as if every cell in her body tuned into the night, and the promise of wondrous things. An unexpected heat began to build low in her belly, flaming out to her fingertips and toes. She had never felt like this, and wasn't sure she liked it.

"Now you have the background. Anything else? I need to go in," she said, pulling her hand free.

"Sure thing, sugar." His hands lifted to her shoulders, where he massaged the tight muscles for a few moments. Then his palms cradled her face between them. Slowly he blocked the stars until his lips touched hers.

Amanda drew in a sharp breath; she had not expected a kiss. His lips closed over hers and he tilted his head slightly to gain better access. Because she had already parted her lips, his tongue met no resistance when it slid across her lower lip, tasting, touching, inflaming. Slowly he eased inside, exploring the warm moist cavern, evoking shimmering shivers that sizzled along every nerve ending.

She had never been kissed like this. Of course, the few dates she had in the past had been with boys.

Hawk was all man. Too much for her, she suspected, but a sudden longing to experience all he had to offer took over and wouldn't let go.

Breathing hard, Hawk pulled back to trail soft kisses across her cheek, down her neck to the pulse point raging out of control at the base of her throat. He licked her skin. She was as sweet as he thought she'd be. Unable to resist, he reclaimed her mouth and again tasted the honey.

She was one soft armful of femininity. His arms banded around her as if he never wanted to let her go. She was sunshine in a dreary life, hot and soft and oh-so-sweet.

Suddenly she pushed hard against his chest. Startled, Hawk let her go.

"I—" With a choked sound, she raced for the door and slammed it shut behind her. He was just like every other man since Bobby Jack. He only wanted one thing! God, wouldn't she ever learn? Her story only gave him the impetus to try. Any respect had fled; he wanted her physically and wasn't hiding the fact, any more than Brent had that morning. She hated this!

Amanda leaned against the hard wooden door and hoped the noise hadn't wakened Joey. Her heart raced a hundred miles an hour. The blood poured through her veins, rushing in her ears so she could hear nothing else. Her skin felt alive with need and want and desire. Her legs were shaky. Tears blurred her vision.

Hawk. She'd just met him a few hours ago and she let him kiss her as if he was her long-lost lover. She blinked her eyes, trying to drive away the moisture that threatened. She was a fool. Acting like that, he'd no more believe she hadn't enticed Bobby Jack than her mother had. She'd practically thrown herself at the man! Not that he was objecting. He had heard enough to believe she was easy. That much was obvious. Hiring him had been a mistake. One she could rectify first thing in the morning. She needed help around the place, not more problems trying to keep her virtue intact.

Her face flaming, she pushed away from the door and headed for her room. She'd take a shower and go to bed. She couldn't change what she'd done, but she didn't have to repeat it. She would never trust a man again. They wanted one thing, took, then moved on.

So saying, the memories of the kiss flooded her mind. Showering did not alleviate the images. Her arms ached to hold that strong body, her fingers yearned to tangle in his thick dark hair, her mouth craved his taste once more. Just once more.

Angry at the inability to stop thinking about that kiss, she snapped off her light and crawled into bed. Into her narrow, lonely bed. She slept nude, but no one knew. She had never slept with a man, had only made love once. And that had proved to be a total disaster. For the millionth heart-stopping moment she wished things were different. Wished *she* were different. That she could take what those randy cowboys offered. Just once. She had the name, why not play the game? But it wasn't just any cowboy she wanted to share her bed with. At last he had a face and a name.

The next morning when Amanda awoke her first thought was to skip breakfast. Walt cooked when she couldn't. But unless she wanted to skip every meal from now until Hawk left, she would only be postponing the inevitable. Slowly she dressed, trying to figure out how she would face him. She figured she knew why he had kissed her, but she couldn't figure out her response. Should she fire him first thing, or see if he would stay and help around the ranch and keep the hell away from her. He'd been the first cowboy to hire on in years and they needed the additional manpower. Yet could she risk keeping him?

She was no closer to an answer when the men stomped in than she had been while dressing. She stacked the hotcakes on the plate and placed the platter in the center of the table. Taking the sausages from the oven where they'd kept warm, she began to serve. Piping hot coffee ready, she filled their cups.

Avoiding Hawk's eyes, she made sure everyone had breakfast before she helped herself. Her nerves were almost shot. Her hand trembled slightly as she speared two pancakes and transferred them to her plate. It took a monumental effort to keep from looking at him. Yet she dared not. She wasn't ready. She still didn't know what to do. But she was aware of every move he made. And it scared her.

She hadn't looked at him once, Hawk thought. And he knew, since he'd had his eyes on her since he'd come in. Not that he blamed her. He had shown as much finesse as a rutting bull last night. Damn, she probably didn't think much more highly about him than she did that Bobby Jack. He had only meant to offer some comfort. He hadn't known it would be so explosive between them. Last night it had taken him several minutes to get his raging hormones under some sort of control. Enough so he could at least walk. He had let the kiss get out of control. Let it? He had been powerless to stop it. But it had been the worst thing he could do, when what he wanted was to gain her trust. To let her know she now had another cowhand on her side.

"You want one of us to stay around to watch Joey when you and Hawk go check out the fencing Standish cut?" Pepe asked as he finished his coffee.

At that, Amanda's eyes met Hawk's. She flushed and looked away, but not before she saw the flare of heat in his. Her heart raced. She'd forgotten they had planned to check the cut fence. She couldn't do it today. Maybe Hawk should ride with Walt.

"No, I think we'll skip—"

"I've already fed the horses and mucked out the stall the mare uses. I'm ready to ride when you are, boss," Hawk interrupted. No way was he going to let her back out. Time they got a few things straight. He hadn't slept much last night. Too wound up after her kiss. So he had plenty of time to think. He thought he'd come up with a way to stop those men, and he planned to use it. But he had to get her to relax enough around him to let him stay, to listen to his plan and cooperate.

"I've got other things to do," she replied shortly.

"They can wait. It won't take us long. I've got an idea."

Intrigued, she met his eyes again, curiosity winning over caution. A willingness to listen winning over her own innate reserve. "What?"

"Let me see the place first, to see if it'll work. I'm ready to ride when you are." He threw out the challenge; would she take it?

Raising her chin, she did. "I'll be ready in half an hour."

"I'll have the horses waiting."

Amanda turned to Pepe. "If you or Walt would watch Joey, we won't be gone long." They'd ride to the wash, assess the damage and return home. Maybe they should take barbed wire and posts with them and repair the damage now. No, that would mean taking the truck and she would rather not be confined in a small space with Hawk Blackstone after last night. She needed more time to get her roiling senses under some sort of control before taking a chance like that.

When she headed for the barn thirty minutes later, Hawk had both horses saddled and loosely tied to the corral fence. He tightened the cinches when she appeared and mounted his horse with a fluid grace.

She noticed he used his saddle on the sorrel gelding. She unhitched her mare and swung up, wishing for the millionth time that she was taller. It was a lot easier to vault flawlessly into the saddle if the stirrup wasn't almost nose high. At least he hadn't used it as an excuse to touch her. She wanted him to keep his distance.

"You lead," Hawk said, holding in his horse.

She headed for the arroyo, conscious of the man riding beside her. She should say something about last night, but didn't know what. It had only been a kiss. Right, like the Tetons in the western part of the state were only a bump in the ground.

Yet if he hadn't felt the same thing from the kiss she had, she'd be an idiot to bring it up. But what if he had? What if he thought because of her response that she might be willing to go a bit further? If so, it was up to her to disabuse him of that notion. She'd be cool, collected and totally businesslike. She had nothing else to offer a cowboy.

Twenty minutes later they came upon the cattle.

She slowed and walked her horse through the small herd grazing in the deep green grass.

"That brand's the running *S*. It's Tom's." She pointed to the rump of one steer.

"And what's the brand for the Royal?"

"A fan with *RF* in the center. Jonas's grandfather wanted cards, but the fan was the best they could get then. We've used it since." She surveyed the cattle. None in this group belonged to her. Shaking her head in disgust, she continued toward the draw.

The wide gully often filled with water in the wettest months, but it was bone dry now. Sloping down, with rocks and scrub narrowing the opening, the cut in the ground spanned forty feet at the narrow point. That was where the wire was cut, the fence posts hacked away. Lips tightened in anger, she studied the opening. On either side, the rocks formed a natural barrier. The fencing on top of the hill stood untouched. It was only in this draw that Tom focused his attentions.

Hawk drew up beside her, dismounted and handed his reins to her. "I want to check out some things," he mumbled, striding away.

She sat on the mare and watched as he walked down to the boundary line. Studying the posts, he picked up some of the strands of barbed wire that had been cut to one-foot lengths. He gathered quite a handful, careful to avoid the barbs.

Standing, he slowly turned, studying the landscape, noting the rocks, the scrub brush, the slope of the draw. He walked over to the left and climbed into the scattered boulders. In seconds he disappeared from view.

Amanda stirred restlessly. What was he doing?

Then he reappeared, still studying the site of the

destruction. Finally he turned and walked back. His hands were empty.

"Where's the wire?" she asked, handing him the reins.

"I left it in the rocks. Cattle won't go there so they can't get cut up. Leave it like it is for today. Tomorrow we'll come and repair it."

"Isn't that for me to decide?" she asked, feeling a need to assert herself.

"So decide to do it tomorrow." Again he effortlessly flowed into the saddle. She watched as he sat as calm as you please on the nervous gelding. He looked as if he'd been born to the saddle. He and the horse moved as one.

"What did you win the saddle for?" she asked, surprising them both.

The left side of his lips moved up in that lazy sexy smile and he met her gaze with his own blue eyes twinkling. If he knew she hadn't meant to ask, he wasn't going to acknowledge it. "Saddle bronc event. Champion at the Houston Rodeo. This was a bonus prize."

"You ride well."

"Eight seconds worth, anyway."

She nodded. "Do you really think you can do something to stop Tom Standish?"

"Oh, yes, sugar, I have the perfect way to stop him." Hawk's voice was low, caressing, reassuring.

Amanda felt it through to her heart. He was going to help her in this. For that she would be forever grateful. One less hassle in life was worth a lot. Maybe the warmth she experienced around him was due to gratitude.

"I think we should repair today," she repeated. "I don't want more of his cattle eating up my grass."

"We won't be ready until tomorrow. No sense in repairing something that could be cut up again. We'll wait."

She wanted to argue, but he hadn't thrown his weight around. He'd stated the sentence calmly and authoritatively. Maybe it was an integral part of his plan. And if there was a chance the repair could be destroyed, he was right, there was no sense in it. She wasn't made of money, and fence posts and wiring cost more than she cared to spend over and over.

Hawk watched her as they headed back for the house. She had put up an invisible wall so high he couldn't even see over it. He knew he had fences of his own to mend with her. But he would not apologize for the kiss. He could hold back, take things slower in the future. He was going to be here for a while; no sense rushing things. He wanted more kisses. Ones that didn't end with her slamming the door between them.

Even though he had thought of little else last night, he could wait a bit longer before kissing her again. At least he hoped he could wait. He had wanted to go over to her at breakfast and steal a quick kiss before eating. All during the meal he'd watched her, his eyes hungry for the sight of her, his body humming with longing. He wished he had dared to help her mount her horse. It stood sixteen hands high and she was a little thing. But watching her mount up had been worth it. The way those jeans had molded her rounded bottom, pulled tight as she swung her leg over, he could just imagine her swinging her legs around him and holding on tight.

Back off! Thinking about her all the time was *not* the way to cool things down. He had enough worries if he wanted to make sure his plan worked. Flexing his hands, he sighed. They were just healing. Still a bit sore. He wondered if horse liniment would aid the healing process.

Time enough to think about courting Amanda Williams later.

Courting!

No. Not courting. That implied commitment and forever. He had already called a real estate firm about a ranch. They were searching Montana and Wyoming right now, trying to locate the perfect property for him. When they called, he'd be leaving.

But until then, he was here and she was here and he wanted her more than any woman he'd ever known.

When they reached the house, Amanda slid off her horse without help and tossed Hawk her reins. "I'll send Pepe out to help unsaddle him." She needed to escape. She'd thought of nothing but Hawk's kiss since they left the arroyo. She had to get her mind on something else before she drove herself crazy, or gave into the longing, threw herself against him and gave credibility to the gossip around town.

"Sure thing, boss." He touched the brim of his hat with one finger and urged the horses to the barn.

She watched him until he was lost from view.

Late in the afternoon Hawk knocked on the screen door to the kitchen. Amanda turned from the roast she placed in the oven and joined him on the porch.

"I need to get into town to pick up a few things. Walt said I should use the truck."

Her heart skipped a beat. "Are you leaving?" Suddenly she realized how much she wanted him to stay. Oh, she knew he'd be leaving when he got tired of working here, or if he got into a fight. But she had just made up her mind to keep him on; she didn't want him to leave. There was so much to do. And in the future, she'd keep herself under control. No more kisses.

Giving in to impulse, Hawk lifted her chin with his finger. "My clothes are in your bunkhouse. My saddle is in your barn. Do you think I'm going to steal the truck and never come back?"

She licked her lips and shook her head slightly. She'd only been afraid he might leave. Why did he touch her so much? She couldn't catch her breath.

"I'll pick up something that will help us stop your neighbor's attacks once and for all. I'll be back before you know it."

"In time for supper?" she asked, her voice whisper soft and husky.

In for an ounce, in for a pound. He was already touching her. What could a little more hurt? Slowly he moved the pad of his thumb until he brushed across the dampness of her lips. Again. She was as soft as a downy newborn calf.

Heat licked along his veins. His jeans grew tight. But he couldn't look away, nor stop his thumb from skimming across her lips. He wanted to cover them again with his own. Taste her again, feel the heat she caused to blaze through him.

"I'll be back in time for supper," he said.

"I leave the keys in the ignition. Drive safely."

She stood stock-still, her eyes wide and silvery in her face. He gazed down into them, feeling as if he were drowning in moonbeams. Reluctantly he withdrew his hand, feeling a chill as he moved away from her. Was this how women enticed men?

He nodded and turned, heading for the truck. Glancing around the yard, he noticed Pepe stood near the water trough, watching them. At least he hadn't given in to the impulse to kiss her. She would have been furious if he had, and even more so if anyone had seen them. But sometime they'd be alone, like last night. And he couldn't guarantee he could stop then.

Amanda watched him drive away, her lips still warm from his touch. He was coming back. He would be here for dinner. She wanted a full update on what he planned to do to stop Tom. Maybe after Joey went to bed she could discuss the plan with Hawk. Would he ask to sit on the swing again?

Or maybe she had better back off far and fast. She'd already had one experience tangling with Bobby Jack. Hawk was more man than Bobby Jack would ever have been. And he naturally thought she was all woman. For heaven's sake, she had a child, didn't she? And a reputation in town that would color anyone's impressions.

But one time provided very limited experiences and nothing to stand up to a randy rodeo cowboy with a hot temper and hotter passions. He was way out of her league and the sooner she recognized it the better. She dare not take a chance on getting hurt. The last time she'd felt something for a man it had left her reputation ruined and her with a child. The entire situation had made an indelible impression. She would never trust a man again, there was too much danger. And she had Joey to think about now.

Four

Amanda spent the afternoon schooling Joey. He was almost finished with the kindergarten curriculum. He could read the simple primers, do easy arithmetic and knew all his shapes and colors. She was proud of her little boy, and enjoyed the hours they spent together in homeschooling.

She watched as he diligently penned the letters he struggled to master. Writing was not a strong suit and she placed more and more emphasis on correct formation of letters. In another week they would be finished the state-mandated material and be free to do other things for the summer. She had purchased workbooks and flash cards the last time she shopped in Thermopolis. Making games of learning fooled Joey into thinking he was only having fun while he learned at a rapid rate.

Gently Amanda reached out and brushed her hand across his head.

"What, Mommy?" he looked up, puzzled.

"Nothing, sweetheart. Just wanted to touch you." She loved him so much it sometimes scared her. Especially after her initial feelings when Bobby Jack had turned on her. She had not wanted to be pregnant. But as the baby developed, and once he was born, she had fallen in love. Even though she saw Bobby Jack's features every day of her life in her son, she loved Joey to distraction. His own sweet personality came through now, and she rarely remembered how much he resembled his father. Joey was his own person. And she'd do all she could to keep him safe.

"How's that?" He held up his paper.

Amanda bent to study the neatly drawn letters. "Perfect!" She reached into the desk drawer and pulled out a packet of stars. Taking a gold one, she placed it at the top of his paper.

His grin melted her heart and she hugged him tightly as she kissed his cheek. He smelled of little boy, and horses and hay.

"Aw, Mommy." He struggled away and rubbed his cheek.

She grinned. "Too much mushy stuff?" she asked.

"Yeah." He smiled at the star on his paper. "I want to show Hawk my paper."

"Hawk's not here right now. He'll be in for supper. You can show him and Walt and Pepe then."

"Okay. Can I go play now?"

"Sure. As soon as you pick up all your things."

"Why? We'll just use them again tomorrow."

"Maybe. I still want the office tidy."

Without further protest, he shoved his papers and

pencils into his drawer. Satisfied with his mother's nod, he ran from the room, anxious to play.

Amanda looked at his paper once again, wondering what Hawk would say when Joey showed him. From the awkward way the man had first spoken to her son she realized he hadn't been around kids much. Though last night on the swing he had seemed more at ease with Joey. Still, he might not want to be bothered by a young child.

She would have to make sure Joey didn't annoy him. Hawk was employed to work on the ranch, not watch Joey. And she didn't want the rugged cowboy to find her son a nuisance.

Hawk didn't seem to find Joey a nuisance at dinner, Amanda thought, watching Hawk and Joey talking. He seemed interested in what the boy had to say, looking directly at him as he spoke, listening intently. She felt a flush of gratitude for the man. Not everyone would give that much consideration to a five-year-old.

Joey basked in the cowboy's attention. He told Hawk about his lessons. "And I got a gold star today. Want to see?"

"I sure do. I got a couple of gold stars myself when I was about your age," Hawk said.

"You did? What for?"

"Spelling. I was a good speller."

"Wow. I can spell some things. C-O-W, cow. And S-T-E-E-R, steer."

"Important words for a rancher to know," Hawk said solemnly.

"I'll get my paper—"

"After we eat, Joey," Amanda interjected, with a

look of apology to Hawk. "The paper's not going anywhere. You can show everyone after dinner."

"But Hawk wants to see it now," Joey protested.

"I can wait. Maybe you can show me where you do your lessons, too," Hawk said.

"Can I, Mommy?"

Amanda smiled and nodded. "After we finish eating." Her gaze flicked to Hawk's, aware of him staring at her. "Thanks."

He shrugged. "I went to school near home. I've never seen a home setup before."

"Boy ought to go to school. Won't know how to mix with others if he doesn't learn in school," Walt grumbled.

"When he's older," Amanda replied. It was a long-standing argument, and one neither would give on. She knew sooner or later Joey had to attend school in town. He had to meet the girls and boys who would one day be his neighbors. But not just yet. He was too young, and the gossip was too rampant. When he was older. When she had found a way to explain things to him.

"Did you get what you wanted in town?" she asked Hawk.

He nodded. "We're all set."

"For what?" Pepe asked.

"Time our neighbors found out we aren't going to sit around idly and let them cut the fences whenever they want, or run their cattle on our land."

Amanda's eyes narrowed, startled at Hawk's referring to her ranch as "our land." She looked at Pepe and Walt. Did they say "our ranch" when talking about the Royal? Why did it bother her when Hawk said it? Just because he arrived yesterday? Or because she didn't trust him?

"Damn straight it's past time. But how you figure to let them know that?" Walt asked, sitting up a little straighter.

"I posted a notice in the feed store, and put an ad in the newspaper, that we're offering grazing land for seven dollars a day per head. Now if your neighbors want to run some head of cattle on our range, we'll just charge them accordingly."

Amanda stared at him. "Are you serious? Can we do that?"

He nodded.

"So we're going to charge for the cattle Standish allowed onto our range?" Walt asked, astonished.

"You bet. I checked out the arroyo this morning with Amanda. That draw is sheltered. A perfect place for people to cut the fence unobserved unless someone else is right in the arroyo. But Standish doesn't run cattle around there. He's got a crop of rocks close to that draw. His cattle didn't wander into our range, they were driven. Mingled in with the cattle hoofprints were those of several horses."

"He won't pay," Amanda said. But she'd love to see his face if Hawk presented him with a bill.

Hawk met her eyes. "Yes, he will," he said softly. "Or he doesn't get his cattle back. I checked with my brother. He's a D.A. down in Cheyenne. He gave me some legal tips."

"Tom will say they wandered. That the fence was not repaired—"

"Ah, but that's where we'll get him," Hawk interrupted.

"How?" Pepe asked. Both older men were leaning

on the table now, fascinated by the direction of Hawk's discussion.

"I let it be known far and wide in town that my first chore since hiring on is to repair downed fences, starting tomorrow. So I figure within the next day or two, Standish will be back to cut the fence, right?"

Three heads nodded, three pairs of eyes never left his face.

"And we'll be waiting for him or his men."

"What?"

"We'll be hidden in the rocks, waiting. When they come, we'll confront them, make sure they know exactly what they are doing and the ramifications."

"And you think they'll meekly turn and never come back?" Amanda asked scathingly. She thought this man might help. For a moment she had thought he could stop the harassment. So far she was less than impressed. Was he planning to *reason* with them?

He winked at her. "Trust me. It'll work."

Scooting back her chair, Amanda stood and began gathering the dishes. "Joey, you take Hawk into the office and show him where you study. Then you can play outside until it gets dark." She had to work to avoid meeting Hawk's gaze, but she did. For a second she had thought he had an idea that would help her. But the man didn't know Tom Standish. His plan was nothing but a puff of air. Even Walt and Pepe mumbled on their way out.

Trust me, he'd said. As if she would trust a man again. Not in this lifetime. She would trust in her own abilities to work through situations. Maybe she'd brick up the arroyo and make sure Tom Standish and his men could never break through.

Or maybe one day they would wear her down and

she'd have to give in and sell. She knew Robert Pembroke would like that. He and Tom were close. For all she knew Robert had put Tom up to bothering her so much she left. After all, they would both benefit. Robert would succeed in running her out of town and Tom would likely buy the ranch at a rock-bottom price.

Her resolve hardened. She would not give in! Maybe, just maybe, Hawk's idea had merit. If not, she'd lived with this kind of petty harassment for more than a year, she could stand it awhile longer. She'd endured the slurs and innuendoes of the cowboys from town a lot longer.

"Good job, Joey. You made these letters perfectly." Hawk sat at the desk, gravely studying the paper Joey held out. "That must have made your Mommy proud."

"Yeah, she kissed me." Unconsciously Joey rubbed his cheek. "Mommy likes that mushy stuff."

Hawk nodded, remembering back when he'd been a boy of five. His mother had already left, so he didn't have a store of memories of mushy stuff. And his father had grown so bitter, he'd spent little time around his son. Hawk had made do with the friends he had at school and Miss Jamison's approval. He'd loved his kindergarten teacher, seeking approval from her that he didn't get at home. But she had never given in to mushy stuff. For all the hardship Amanda faced, her son still looked like a well-adjusted, happy kid.

"Mommies are good for that," Hawk agreed. "Do you like homeschooling? Do you wish you could go to school in town?" Why was the boy being homeschooled? Was transportation a problem? Or was it the school system itself?

"I never get to go to town. Maybe when I'm older," Joey replied.

Hawk smiled. That last sounded like a quote. "I can take you in with me someday, if you like. Maybe even get an ice-cream cone."

"Really, Hawk? I never get to go. I want a chocolate ice cream."

"We'll have to ask your mother first."

"Mommy, Mommy." Joey ran from the room and Hawk could hear his excited voice all the way from the kitchen.

Two minutes later Amanda stood in the doorway, her eyes flashing, her hands on her hips. "Joey does not need to go into town. And don't be giving him ideas!" she said shortly.

Hawk looked up, startled. "It's no problem for me to take him in next time I go. I could buy him an ice-cream cone."

"No."

"Afraid I'll kidnap the boy?" he asked silkily, rising to his full height and crossing the room. Anger flared as he met the glare in her eye. What did she think he was going to do with her son?

"Of course not." She dismissed the notion with a quick shake of her head. "It has nothing to do with you. I don't want Joey in town."

"Until he's older," Hawk said.

"Right."

"Why?"

"Come on, Hawk, you're a smart man. What do you think the gossips will say to my son?"

He raised his eyebrows in surprise. "You think anyone would say something to a child?"

She nodded.

"I doubt it. They don't even have to know who he is, if he goes in with me."

"Even if they don't say it to him directly, there could be talk where he'd hear it. He's my baby, Hawk, and I don't want anything to hurt him."

"Sugar, you can't live his life for him. You can't make sure he gets through life without some hurts. Sooner or later—"

"Then let it be later. He's too young to hear malicious gossip about his mother."

Hawk stared at her for a long moment. "Maybe that's something else we should try to change," he said slowly.

"Another great idea, like listing grazing rates and expecting Tom Standish to stop cutting my fence?" she retorted.

He shook his head, his eyes a deep dark blue, never leaving hers. "No. This might take a bit more time. I'll think on it."

"Right, you do that. But in the meantime, Joey doesn't go into town, agreed?"

"You're his mother."

She nodded and turned away. She may be Joey's mother, but when around Hawk, she felt more like a young girl giddy with the attention of an older man. She frowned as she walked back into the kitchen. She didn't want any kind of emotional baggage with Hawk. Pushing open the screen door, she went to sit on the back steps, spotting Joey near the corral. She smiled. Her son was horse mad. One day she'd have to find a pony for him. He was old enough to learn to ride, and he dropped enough hints.

Maybe Hawk would teach him. She shook her head. She could teach her own son.

Hawk sat at the desk for a few minutes, considering all he'd found out about Amanda Williams. Rising, he went to find her. In seconds he was through the back door, and standing beside her. He didn't know what he was doing, but he felt antsy, wanting to do something. He didn't know the full story. She'd given her side of what happened, but he hadn't heard Bobby Jack's. And never would. Was she telling the truth, or had she fancied it up to make her seem the victim? In his experience women were more than able to take care of themselves. And take the male in their life for a ride. Had she tried to seduce Bobby Jack and it backfired on her? Was she looking for something from him that she hadn't found elsewhere?

Or was her story true? There was an innocent bewilderment about her that gave him pause every time he thought he'd figured her out.

"Amanda?"

Every nerve ending in her body went to full attention. She closed her eyes briefly, snapped them open lest he suspect her reaction to just hearing his deep voice. She turned and looked up, way up. His gaze was brooding, his eyes narrowed, the muscles in his cheeks clenched.

"Are you angry?" she asked. He sure looked it. She shivered. She hoped he wasn't angry at her. Involuntarily she glanced at his hands, the knuckles still bruised from some fight he'd had before he arrived in Tagget.

"A bit." He lowered himself until he sat on the

step below hers. His head was on a level with hers and Amanda could see the tiny lines radiating from his eyes, see the bruise along his jaw, the day's worth of beard on his cheeks. Her fingers longed to skim along the bruise and touch the prickle of his beard. She wondered what it would feel like against her fingertips, against her mouth.

Looking away, heat suffused. She had to work to draw in breath. "Why?" She needed him to talk, needed him to give her something else to think about besides him.

"I'm angry you're letting these people buffalo you. You and your son have a perfect right to wander into town anytime you want."

"What?" She hadn't expected something like that. Looking at Hawk, she shook her head. "You don't know what it's like. Bobby Jack's precious family closed ranks, and they are the most powerful people in town. If the ranch had a mortgage, I'm sure the bank would have foreclosed. I can't get credit anywhere—it's cash and carry all the way. I get harassed every time. You saw the men at the diner, and in the feed store. It's like that most times. I avoid Tagget as much as I can and I sure don't want my son going in."

"This has been going on for six years?"

"Not exactly. After…after I came to live with Jonas, I didn't go into town. I think things died down. But when Jonas was so sick, I had to go in to buy things. I ran into Bobby Jack just before he was killed. He taunted me, made all sorts of lewd suggestions, and when I blew up, he just laughed and then it started again. I guess he got his friends to spread the word once more. Anyway, ever since then, I hate to go to town.''

''How did he die?''

''Dead drunk. He wrapped his truck around a tree,'' she said succinctly.

''Hell of a legacy to pass on to his son.''

''Joey doesn't know about his father,'' she said quickly.

''Another thing to keep from him until he's older?'' Hawk asked.

Her eyes met his. ''You may not agree with how I'm raising my child, but that's how I'm doing it. I don't need your approval.'' She could feel the heat from his body against her leg, her side. More disturbed than she was willing to admit, she fisted her hands and dropped them between her legs to refrain from giving in to the temptation to reach out and touch him.

She didn't need his approval, but she would have liked it. Would have liked to have him praise her and look at her with admiration in his eyes.

''Sugar, I think you're doing a fine job. Only, sometimes it's better for a person to learn something when he's young. That way he won't have the shock of having his life turned upside down later.''

She considered his words. ''Like finding out you're adopted at age eighteen or something.''

''Yeah, something like that. What do you tell him when he asks about his father?''

''He doesn't ask.''

''That's not natural. He's asking someone and I bet it's Pepe or Walt. They've probably told him not to talk to you about it.''

''So I'm supposed to tell him his father was a

drunken, womanizing ne'er-do-well and his mother is the town slut so he doesn't have to wonder anymore?'' she asked scathingly.

He reached out and pressed two fingers against her lips. ''His mother is not the town slut. One thing that gets me real riled is injustice. As I see it, we've got a major case of it right here. Time you stood up for yourself, sugar, and stop hiding away, stop ignoring the gossip, and tell the world the truth.''

Her hand circled his wrist and she pulled his hand away. She could feel the steady beat of his pulse beneath her fingers. She leaned forward a little, feeling the brush of his breath on her cheek. She felt enveloped by Hawk. His skin was warm beneath her fingertips, his presence comforting, even if the topic of conversation disturbed her.

''I tried telling the truth. That's what got me into this situation. I should have just quietly gone away, had the baby and given him up, like my mother said.''

''Nothing personal, but I don't think your mother was the best in the world.'' Not that he could talk. His mother hadn't even hung around long enough for him to know if she was good or not. At least Amanda had a mother of sorts while growing up.

''I don't, either, but she was all I had.'' The betrayal when she had most needed support had cut deep. Amanda couldn't understand her mother. She knew she would never reject Joey, no matter what happened to him, no matter what he did.

''Where is she now?'' he asked.

''Phoenix. She moved there five years ago.''

''When Joey was born?''

''Just before, actually.'' She licked her lips. She was losing track of the conversation, lost in the deep blue of Hawk's eyes. She hadn't talked about her life before and it made her uneasy. She tried to ignore the bad aspects, and concentrate on the good. Which was Hawk, good or bad?

"Amanda," he said softly, slipping his wrist from her hand, turning to clasp it with his.

"What?" She swallowed hard. He planned to kiss her again. She knew it. There was plenty of time to stop it. He wasn't forcing her. But she didn't move. Or did she lean forward just another inch?

His lips were warm and firm against hers. He moved them gently, coaxingly. Sighing softly, she responded. When his tongue traced the seam, she opened her mouth and almost moaned in delight at the sensations that splashed through her at his touch. His free hand came up to cup the back of her head, tilting her slightly to better access her mouth. His tongue plunged in, exploring, tantalizing, enticing.

Amanda gave in to the yearning that had plagued her and ran her fingertips gently against his jaw, relishing the feel of his masculine scruff. The yearning grew and changed. She wanted to feel him against her neck, her shoulders, her breasts. She wanted to feel all of him against all of her.

Startled, she pulled back, her eyes wide. "I can't do this," she whispered, surprised she even began to think she would desire a man. Look what happened the last time.

"I think you kiss very well," he said softly, his hand still holding her head, his fingers rubbing across the softness of her hair. He wanted to see it released from the braid, spread around her shoulders, framing her face. He wanted to run his fingers through it over and over, to have the silky weight lay on his chest, his arms.

He wanted her.

Amanda saw the flare of desire in Hawk's gaze and tried to look away, tried to breathe, tried to slow the rapid gallop of her heart. But she couldn't move. She could only stare at the man who had captured her attention, who made her body ache with longing, and wonder where she was going to get the strength to run away.

"I'm not going to be beguiled into forgetting who I am. I refuse to get tangled up with some man again. Especially some itinerant hot-tempered cowboy who just breezes in and thinks he can hop into my bed!" She pushed against his shoulder and he released her. Scooting across the step, Amanda put in as much distance as she could before standing.

"You're here to work my ranch, not work on me. Or are you starting to believe the talk in town?"

He rose with a surge and in two steps towered over her. His anger was almost tangible. "Grow up, little girl. You're acting like an outraged Victorian virgin, which we both know damn well you are not! There's nothing wrong with a kiss between consenting adults. And, sugar, you were as consenting as hell. You're not sixteen anymore, Amanda. And I never said a word about getting into your bed!" With that, he turned and stalked away.

Amanda watched him, her heart beating so fast she was afraid it would burst from her chest. She couldn't believe she'd said what she had. She couldn't believe she would react so strongly to a kiss. It had been more than she'd ever expected and her emotions were in turmoil. She wasn't used to this. She hadn't dated in six years. She didn't know how men and women reacted, only how she reacted being near Hawk. And it scared her down to her toes.

Right after a rather stilted breakfast the next morning, Amanda stacked the dishes in soapy water and turned to follow the men from the kitchen. The air was cool, the sky clear. It would be a hot day once the sun had a chance to warm up.

"Did you pack lunches?" Walt asked as they crossed the yard toward the barn.

"What? No, we'll be finished by noon, we can eat back here." She gazed uneasily toward the barn. Hawk had left the house as soon as he'd finished eating. He had already loaded the pickup truck with the barbed wire, poles and shovels. He would be back out again in a minute. She still hadn't spoken directly to him. Wiping her palms against her jeans, she waited to see him again.

Hawk came out of the barn carrying two tool cases. He glanced at Amanda and Walt, his look coolly impersonal. Dumping the cases into the back of the pickup truck, he turned back to Amanda.

"Any instructions, boss?"

She could see the anger. So she had panicked last night. He couldn't still be mad about that, could he?

"I'm going," she said, readjusting her hat firmly on her head. She met his gaze, her own steady and determined.

"You're the boss," he said through tight lips.

Pepe came from the barn carrying the fasteners and the hammers. He looked at the three standing near the truck. "Something up?" he asked.

"No. Ready to ride?" Hawk climbed in behind the

wheel and slammed his door. He started the engine and sat glaring out the windshield. The temperature seemed to drop fifteen degrees.

Amanda looked at Pepe and then sighed. Maybe this wasn't such a good idea. She opened the passenger door and gingerly sat in the bench seat, sliding across until she almost touched Hawk. Pepe climbed in after her.

"Scoot over a bit more, boss. I can't get the door closed."

More? As in even closer to Hawk?

She scooted even closer, until her hip touched his, her left thigh felt the heat from his right one. She swallowed hard, remembering her words from last night. Remembering his kiss. Walt was right, Pepe and Hawk could have handled the repairs without her. Did she fool anyone but herself? She didn't need to ride along to make sure things were done correctly. She knew enough from the references she'd called that Hawk would do a perfect job. She knew enough from just being around him that he would do his best. He never did less.

But she was going—it was too late to get out of the truck without making an even bigger fool of herself. And that she dare not do. Not in front of Hawk Blackstone.

Pepe closed his door. "Ready to roll."

Five

Hawk pulled up and stopped with a small ridge between them and the damaged fence. The truck couldn't get down into the draw, but he pulled as close as he could. Scanning the area, he cut the engine. The next time he came he would park back under that cottonwood. That way the vehicle would be hidden from view. Because the next time he came it would be to stop the fence cutting, and he wouldn't want to give away the show.

Pepe opened his door and hopped out, going to the back and picking up several of the fence posts. Balancing them on his shoulder, he headed for the arroyo.

Amanda reached out and touched Hawk's arm before he could get out. He froze, then turned and looked at her.

"I'm sorry about last night," she said in a soft

voice. Her grip tightened. "I was out of line and I apologize."

He stared at her, wondering what brought on the apology. She'd been sure enough last night.

"You have no reason to apologize, Ms. Williams. You made yourself clear last night." And if he had a hope of keeping his sanity around her, he had better remember every word she'd flung at him.

"I was scared," she admitted, coloring up.

He started; that was the last thing he expected to hear from her. And yet he should have seen it. He'd spent most of the night trying to rationalize away the scene on the back porch. And her being scared had been one aspect.

"I'm not Bobby Jack, or those other cowboys in town," he stated between clenched teeth. Anger simmered just beneath the surface. All because she had lumped him in the same group as those men in town. He wasn't like that and she should have instantly recognized it.

"I know you're not. I'm sorry. I can't say anything more. I shouldn't have accused you of that. You were right—I was a willing participant in the kiss." More than willing, eager for it. "I don't have a lot of experience with man-woman things." She dropped her hand, gazed out the window. Color stained her cheeks. This was so awkward!

Of course she didn't have any experience. Her one foray into love had ended disastrously. She had shunned men since. He was wrong in his accusation last night. She *was* just like a Victorian virgin, and he'd best remember that if he wanted to get anywhere with his pretty boss.

He opened his door. "Apology accepted, though

not needed.'' Standing, he moved to the side of the pickup and gathered the barbed wire and post-hole digger. Striding across the rocky soil, he tried to ignore the thoughts spinning around in his head. He didn't want to get anywhere with his boss. He was putting in time while waiting to buy a spread of his own. One that was up-to-date and wasn't falling down around his ears like the Royal Flush.

He would call the real estate agent when he got back to the bunkhouse. See if anything looked promising. Urge the man to hurry and find something.

Amanda watched him walk over the rise. If she had expected her apology to work miracles, she was doomed to disappointment. Amanda climbed down from the pickup cab and reached into the back to get the hammers. She scooped up the box of fasteners and slowly followed. She'd only known the man a couple of days and already missed the companionship that had sprung up between them. What could she do to make things go back the way they had started?

When she reached the property line, Pepe and Hawk had already pulled out the damaged posts and were discussing where to dig the new holes. She scanned the area, wondering how long after they finished the repair Tom Standish would send his men.

The day grew warm as they worked. Amanda wished she'd worn short sleeves. The men had it easier. When it got too hot, they took off their shirts.

And that made her even warmer.

Hawk's chest was strong and wide, his shoulders and arms muscular, attesting to the hard physical work he did. His skin was darkly tanned. Obviously he often worked without his shirt. She could see bruises along his left ribs. Even with the injuries from his recent fight, he still worked twice as hard as Pepe.

Amanda couldn't take her eyes off him. She handed him the fasteners when he asked for them, held the hammer when he pulled the wire taut, fascinated by the muscles moving in his arms, his back. Her eyes never left his body. She wanted to feel those muscles move. Wanted to touch him to see how his skin felt. A sheen of moisture coated him. Did that keep his skin cool, or was he hot to touch?

Hawk stopped and stared at her. She looked up, her gaze ensnared with his. The angles and planes of his face shone in sharp relief in the sun, his hat shaded his eyes. But she could feel the intensity of his gaze.

"Pepe, go to the truck and see if you can find the wire cutters," Hawk said, holding Amanda's gaze.

"Sure thing."

She heard Pepe walk away, his footsteps fading as he climbed the hill and disappeared over the top.

"If you don't stop looking at me like you could eat me up, I can't get anything done," Hawk said harshly.

She smiled. "That describes it, I guess."

He took a step closer. "Describes what?"

"What I'm feeling around you." Her voice never faltered. She took a step closer and reached out to trail her fingers down his biceps. She wanted to touch his chest, but wasn't quite that brave.

"Amanda, after last night—"

"I was wrong last night, I already apologized. Please, Hawk, don't hold that against me."

"What I want to hold against you is me," he growled, pulling her into his arms and covering her mouth with his.

It was glorious, as she'd known it would be. His skin felt slick and hot and taut over well-defined muscles. His chest was as unyielding as the rocks that were scattered around them. Yet his touch was gentle, his mouth coaxing. She responded like kindling to a match, giving as well as receiving.

She reveled in the pleasure that coursed through her, delighted in the shocking sensations his hands brought as they roamed around her body, pressing her closer, cupping her bottom to bring her even tighter to him. She felt the hard ridge of his desire, stunned at the heady reaction of her own body. He wanted her, she knew that much. And she wanted him. It scared her, but it also enthralled her as nothing else had ever done.

He pushed her back, held her shoulders, his fingers caressing. "Pepe's coming back," he said, his eyes glittering with suppressed emotion. His breathing was fast, and Amanda smiled at the proof she wasn't the only one affected by that earth-shattering kiss.

By the time Pepe crested the rise, Hawk stood several feet away.

"Sorry, Pepe, I found it just after you left." Hawk held up the wire cutters, then proceeded to cut the end of the roll.

Pepe glanced at Amanda, then sharply at Hawk. He said nothing, but his expression became thoughtful.

"Who's the cowboy on the ridge?" Hawk asked a few minutes later.

Amanda looked up. In the distance, on the ridge of Standish's land, a lone cowboy sat on a horse, watching them.

"I can't tell from here. One of Tom's men, I'm sure."

Hawk smiled in satisfaction. "Good. He'll report back that the fence is repaired. Within the next day or so the cutters should be back."

"This constant repairing of the fence costs money, you know," she mentioned.

"The next time will be the last time," Hawk said, keeping an eye on the cowboy as they finished.

He hesitated a moment as he pulled on his shirt, studying the surrounding hills. When the cowboy rode slowly away, he turned toward Pepe. "My guess is they won't come today. Probably already assigned their chores. But tomorrow, maybe."

"And we do what, Hawk?"

"We wait for them. We'll hide in these rocks until they actually cut a strand. Then we catch them in the act."

"And that'll make them stop?" Amanda said. "They'll laugh in our faces."

"Maybe not." He planned personally to make sure Tom Standish got the message they would not tolerate further trouble.

"I can't wait till you tell Tom he can't get his cattle back unless he pays grazing fees," she mumbled as they walked back to the truck.

He smiled. "Me, too."

She looked exasperated. "Hawk, it won't work. He's got ten or more cowboys who do his bidding. He's got the sheriff on his side, and Robert Pembroke."

"And you have the law on your side. This is the 1990s not the 1890s. We're not Johnson County and there's not going to be a range war. Trust me on this, sugar."

"Right." The only man she'd ever trusted had

been Jonas. She didn't think it was in her to trust someone else. Especially someone who sent such mixed messages. One minute calmly discussing the ranch, the next trying to kiss her senseless, then telling her he planned to leave first chance he got. As soon as the realty company found him a ranch, he was gone.

There was nothing to trust.

I ride for the brand.

She smiled. It sounded so old-fashioned. Did that mean he would expend every effort while employed on the Royal Flush on her behalf? She began to think so. Or was she setting herself up for a huge heartbreak?

Heartbreak? No! She was not talking affairs of the heart. Only ranch business. The rest—the kisses, the touches—were a way to pass the time. She was not going to fall for some transient cowboy, no matter how much desire she felt around him. She knew better than to trust a man with her heart. Never again would she venture that.

She might even believe it if she could stay away from him.

That afternoon she worked with Joey. After he finished the day's lessons, she sent him outside to play while she caught up on the accounting for the ranch. She sighed when she saw her bank balance. She desperately needed the extra worker, but paying Hawk would put a big dent into a small balance. She'd have to sell more cattle. She got tired of this balancing act. Things would be better if she could run a credit at the local stores, sell her cattle at the optimum price, like the other ranchers did. But that wasn't the way things went. She could still manage, though. And with Hawk's help, she could pull things around, get more done, build up the ranch.

When she went to fix dinner, Amanda checked out the kitchen window and saw her son following Hawk around. The two of them were deep in conversation and she longed to know what they were discussing. Her heart warmed as she watched Hawk talk with her son, stoop down to his level to say something very serious. Joey nodded and then the two of them walked into the barn and were lost from view.

She hoped Joey wasn't being a pest. But somehow she thought Hawk able to take care of himself. If he didn't want Joey around, he could tell the boy.

Of course, Joey would be entranced with Hawk. The man was much younger than Walt or Pepe or Jonas. He did things differently. Amanda hadn't found anything that would prevent him from being a perfect role model for Joey. For as long as he stayed, she reminded herself. Was there a danger Joey would become *too* attached to the man? If so, he'd be heartbroken when Hawk left. Why wasn't life easy?

Hawk smiled down at the boy following him. He hadn't spent much time around kids, but Joey was fun. Hawk especially liked the ideas in the youngster's head, and the funny questions he asked. He was a bright boy, eager to learn. Hawk was touched that Joey wanted to learn from him. Maybe it would be worth getting married if he could have some kids.

Though he wouldn't go into a marriage like his father had, expecting love, expecting forever. If he did get married, he would make sure it was a business deal, clean and simple with everything spelled out up front. If the woman ever left, she'd get nothing from his ranch. And the children would stay with him. Knowing up front that his wife might leave would insure he didn't become the bitter man his father had been.

"—ride," Joey finished.

"What was that, partner?" Hawk hadn't heard the last sentence.

"If you go out on your horse you can take me to ride," Joey repeated impatiently. "Couldn't you?"

"Does your mother allow that?" Hawk asked, reaching the stall door. He had planned to groom the horse and ride out toward the river, check on some of the cattle. There was still a couple of hours until dinner; he had time.

"I can ask her," Joey said.

"Go make sure it's all right. It is with me, if it is with your mother."

Joey turned and ran as fast as his little legs allowed. Hawk smiled after the kid. Turning to groom his horse he wondered at the changes in his life the past few days. Who would have thought on his birthday just a week ago that he'd be championing a single mother, teaching ranching to a five-year-old and plotting ways to stop a vengeful rancher from exacting his plans? And he was still trying to think of a way to change the town's opinion of Amanda.

It would all be a job well done, if he could pull it off before he left. He heaved the saddle on the horse. Maybe he'd hold off calling the real estate agent for another day or two. No rush on getting a place of his own. He'd like to get everything squared away here before leaving. And God knew there was ton of work to be done around the Royal.

He wondered if lack of manpower was the only thing holding Amanda back. The house needed repair and paint, the barn could use a few new shingles, the corral needed some new rails and the hinges on the gate were on their last legs. From his brief survey of the range, water holes needed cleaning and the miles of fencing needed to be patrolled. She needed more than the three men she now employed. She needed—

"She said yes!" Joey came flying back inside the barn, his face almost split in two by his grin. "She said yes, Hawk. I can go!"

"Great, partner. Let's ride." Hawk lifted the boy into the saddle and made sure he held on to the horn while he led the horse outside. Mounting behind Joey, Hawk held him firmly against him as they began to move.

"Yippee!" Joey yelled, wiggling around in his excitement.

"Easy, partner, don't want to spook the horse. Settle down and we'll put him in a lope." Giving the command, Hawk set the horse at the lope and the two of them rode to check out the cattle.

"And then we went really fast, Mommy. Faster than in the truck, right, Hawk?" Joey glanced at Hawk as they sat around the table, everyone listening to Joey recount his afternoon ride.

"Right."

Amanda smiled at him, then turned her attention back to her son. She hadn't seen him this animated in a long time.

"And then we saw the cattle. And we looked at

the mama cows and the baby calves. But we didn't see any of the daddy cows, did we, Hawk?''

''No.''

''And then we…'' He trailed off and turned to Hawk. ''Then what?''

''Then we checked out the grazing potential in that stretch of range.''

''Yes. And then what?''

''Then we checked the water holes.''

''Yes and then, Mommy, we looked for gophers so we didn't step on any and break the horse's knees.''

Hawk coughed gently and looked away. Close enough. He wouldn't want to step on any gophers any more than he wanted to step in a gopher hole. He hadn't known the routine ride would have engendered so much enthusiasm. He caught Amanda's grateful smile and smiled back at her. She looked pretty watching her boy recount his afternoon. Her cheeks held color, her eyes were silvery gray. He wished she'd undone her hair. One day before he left he planned to run his fingers through it.

''Sounds like you've the real makings of a rancher,'' Walt said, enjoying the boy's tale.

''Right. Hawk says a rancher has to always know his stock, and his range. He has to be prepared for all…all…'' Joey looked at his hero. ''What do ranchers have to be prepared for?''

''All eventualities.''

Joey frowned at the big word and his mother laughed softly. ''That's right, Joey, so pay attention when Hawk shows you something.''

''I loved riding the horse,'' he ended.

''But you stay away from him when an adult isn't around,'' Hawk said. ''Geronimo is too big. He might not see you around him and step on you or something.''

"I know." Joey's face dropped a bit as he began eating again.

Amanda felt a pang. She would have to get him a pony. Time he learned to ride. If she got a docile one, he could groom it, play with it, ride it in the corral and then ride out with one of the men if they had the time to watch him.

And she and he could ride together. She would teach him all she knew about her quarter horses and expand his education in ranching.

Tomorrow she'd call around. Someone must have a pony for sale. She knew she couldn't really afford it, but she'd sacrifice anything for her son's happiness.

"Mighty fine eating, Amanda," Walt said as he shoved his plate away.

"Glad you liked it, Walt." She smiled.

"Are you going to sit with Mommy on the swing now?" Joey asked Hawk.

Amanda reached for the empty plates, rising quickly to avoid any appearance of waiting to hear Hawk's answer.

"Not tonight, partner. There are some saddles that need some work. Thought I'd soap them while watching TV. Pepe and Walt are going to help me. Want to help, too?"

"Yes!" Joey scrambled from his chair. "Can I go help with the saddles, Mommy?" he asked, dancing around the kitchen in his excitement.

"Sure." She glanced at Hawk, hoping her disappointment didn't show. It wasn't as if she had expected him to spend the evening with her. She had things to do. And it would be a relief to have Joey entertained. "Send him in around eight. He needs a bath before bed."

"Right." Hawk started to say something, thought better of it and left, Joey walking proudly at his side.

When the dishes were washed and put away, Amanda wandered out to the front porch and sank onto the swing. She wished Hawk had wanted to spend the time with her. There was no denying that. She could put on a good front before him and the others, but deep inside she had hoped he'd want to sit with her and talk.

She brought one foot up to the edge of the swing, used the other to push back and forth. Resting her cheek on her bent knee, she tried to figure out her tangled emotions. He wanted her, she knew that. But she didn't get the same feelings around him that she did around the cowboys she ran into in town. They all wanted her, but just to sleep with. To brag about another notch on their bedposts.

Hawk talked to her. He treated her as if she were a real person, not just a body. He took his job seriously and worked hard.

And he kissed like nothing in this world.

She frowned. There was nothing wrong with kissing. Men and women did it all the time. It didn't necessarily lead to bed. Though she wouldn't mind— No! She'd made a big mistake as a teenager; she wouldn't tempt fate a second time.

But for a few minutes she daydreamed that Hawk loved her. That he wanted to stay with her, work on the Royal and build it up until its reputation as a horse breeding ranch became outstanding. That together they'd have children to raise, to love, to leave the ranch to. She would have liked more children. She loved Joey. A daughter would be nice. Or another sturdy little boy.

But even nicer would be to have a husband who loved her. Who shared the burden of the ranch so she wasn't so alone. Who would tease her and laugh with her and turn her to mush when he kissed her. She sighed. Dreams were a foolish way to spend her time. There was too much else to do, and too little money with which to do it.

And tomorrow they were spending the day hidden in the rocks to catch a fence cutter.

Amanda settled her hat, tilting it to keep the early sun from her eyes. They had arrived a half hour ago. Hawk had stationed Walt and her in a different area, close to the fence, behind boulders, hidden from view. He had surprised her with one of those disposable cameras. His instructions had been explicit.

She was to take pictures from the moment the man dismounted, through each step until she had everything on film. He'd take care of the rest.

Nothing had happened yet. Growing bored, Amanda began to mentally list all the tasks that needed doing. The most critical ones first, like riding the rest of the perimeter fencing. Then the cross fencing. She needed to inspect the mares and see how the new foals were doing. Walt had checked every day this week, but she missed being with her horses and wanted to see for herself.

Then there was the hay. She tried to grow her own to supplement her feed demands in winter. The first cut was due in the summer, but she wanted to see how it was growing. It took a bit of scheduling, getting a cutter in from Thermopolis, rather than from

Tagget, but no one in town would cut her hay. Most of them owed money at the bank and were more than agreeable to fall in with Robert Pembroke's embargo.

A noise caught her attention. Carefully she drew her hat off her head and rose up enough to peer over the edge of the boulder. Riding down on the far side were two men. As they drew closer, she recognized Matt Billings, one of Tom Standish's men. The other cowboy was a stranger, but she knew he worked for Tom, as well. Hawk had been right; they had come the day after the repair.

Slowly she brought up the bright yellow camera, staying as low as she could. Peering through the viewfinder, she centered the men and pressed the button. The clicking as she advanced the film sounded loud in her ears, but the two men didn't appear to notice. They were too intent on their task.

In only seconds, Matt had dismounted, drawn wire cutters from his back pocket and snipped the top two strands of barbed wire. Amanda caught it all on film.

"That's enough." Hawk stood and strode out from the rock he'd been behind, his face tight with anger, his eyes narrowed and mean. He walked easily to the fence, facing Matt, his hands loose at his sides, his manner deceptively calm.

"Destroying other people's property is against the law, boys," Hawk drawled.

Matt hesitated a minute, then deliberately snipped the third strand. "That so?" he taunted. "This fence was down last week. Some of our cattle wandered across. We're just getting them back."

"It was down because you cut it down. You're not getting any cattle today."

"And who's going to stop us?" Matt scanned the area, seeing no one, and faced Hawk again. "You?"

"If it comes down to that."

"Hey, man, what's the deal? You trying to impress your boss lady? Shouldn't take that much. She seemed willing yesterday. Is she as hot between the sheets as the other guys in town say she is?" Matt smirked.

Hawk moved so fast Amanda was stunned. He stepped across the remaining strands of fence, chopped his hand against Matt's arm. The wire cutters flew away. Taking two fistfuls of shirt, Hawk slammed Matt against his horse. The animal whinnied in fright, sidestepping away. Hawk never released his grip, his face blazing with anger.

"If you ever say one more disrespectful word about Amanda Williams, I will personally see to it that you lose your teeth so you can't slander anyone again. Do I make myself clear?" His voice was whiplash hard, dangerous. The strength displayed while he held Matt as if he were a rag doll staggered Amanda. Stunned, she couldn't believe her eyes and ears.

"Yes." Matt's voice came out low, a trace of fear evident.

"I can't hear you."

"I said yes." Matt cleared his throat, his eyes wide, his gaze never leaving Hawk's. "But everyone knows—"

"Everyone knows damn all, as far as I can tell. The woman is a lady to her toes. If you ever hear of anyone saying differently, you let me know. I'll take care of them the same as I'll take care of you if you ever malign her name again."

"Hey, man, I didn't mean anything." Matt swallowed hard. "I won't say anything again."

Slowly Hawk felt the white-hot anger fade. He released his grip on the cowboy's shirt. He wanted to smash his fist into his face, make the man grovel for his words about Amanda.

He would have to make do with what he got. Matt glanced nervously back at the other rider.

"Give your boss a message from the Royal Flush Ranch," Hawk said evenly, only his clenched fists displaying the angry emotions that had not totally dissipated. "Tell him we have today's illegal fence cutting on film. If he trespasses on Royal Flush land again, we will prosecute to the fullest extent of the law."

Matt looked shocked. He glanced around. Amanda stood, holding the camera clearly in view. She wanted to laugh aloud at Matt's expression, but kept her own serious. For a moment the triumph was wonderful. She wasn't sure how long it would last, but it was heady now.

"We have cattle on your range," the other rider said. "We need to get them back."

"Tom Standish can call to discuss the fees for grazing on our land. We'll return the cattle once he's paid," Hawk replied.

"You can't—" Matt slumped down at the hard look Hawk turned on him. "All right, I'll tell him." He turned to his horse.

"Hold on. Before you go, repair that fence." Hawk caught his shoulder and spun him around.

Working with some of the small cut pieces from before, Matt and Jeremy Strothers, the second cowboy, had the fence repaired within ten minutes. Hawk,

Walt and Amanda watched as the men worked quickly and efficiently. Only when they had ridden out of sight did Hawk turn and start back toward the truck.

Amanda grabbed her hat and jogged down the slope, intercepting him. She threw her arms around his neck and kissed him. Smiling up brightly, her emotions bubbled and churned.

"Thank you, Hawk Blackstone. No one has ever stood up for me before. I will treasure that memory for the rest of my days!"

His arms came around her, his hands on her waist. She was so slim and dainty. How could she draw the energy to face every day with such enthusiasm? Yet she was strong, he could feel her strength in her arms as they drew him closer. Elegant femininity around steely strength, a heady combination.

"I'll wait in the truck," Walt mumbled as he walked by.

"We'll be right there," Hawk said, his head lowering to Amanda's. He pressed his lips against hers, feeling the surge of desire he now expected around her. She was a lady from top to toe, as he'd told the cowboy. He, himself, had best never forget that.

Conscious of Walt waiting, he kept the kiss short. Too short, Hawk thought when he forced himself to release the sweet armful. He took off his hat, dragging his fingers through his hair. She was potent, too much for him if he wanted to keep his hands to himself. The thought of her tempted him night and day.

Amanda turned and started for the truck feeling as if she was floating. And it wasn't all because of the successful confrontation with Standish's men. She licked her lips, tasting Hawk. Her heart pounded. She felt as if she were ten feet tall. No one had ever stood up for her before. Granted, Jonas had offered her a place to stay and a job, but he hadn't threatened anyone to stop spreading the gossip.

She felt special, for a moment almost cherished. And it was all because of Hawk Blackstone.

Six

"**D**o you really think Tom Standish will call to ransom his cattle?" Amanda asked as she sat between Hawk and Walt in the truck. They bounced over the field, heading back for the ranch house.

"We'll see. We need to get the film developed, make sure the pictures are good."

"Better do it in Thermopolis, then. I'd hate for something to 'accidentally' happen to this roll," Amanda said dryly.

"Wouldn't put it past anyone," Walt said. "Time to schedule the hay cutter, anyway. You can kill two birds with one stone."

"What about the hay cutter?" Hawk asked.

"I hire a firm from Thermopolis. Can't get anyone locally. Last year they promised, then didn't show up. Claimed it was a scheduling problem. But by that time it was almost too late. I was lucky to get Harrison and Sons from Thermopolis."

"Jonas had no problems before?"

"No, but then he wasn't me."

"I'll take the film in to be developed," Hawk said as he pulled up beside the barn.

"I want to go, too."

"Bring Joey and we'll make it a special outing for him."

She looked at Hawk. "I have taken him into Thermopolis before."

"I didn't think you'd kept him incarcerated here his entire life." He smiled at her, his eyes dancing in amusement at her huffy attitude.

"It's not exactly incarceration," she replied heatedly.

He chuckled and flicked her shoulder. "Knock off the chip, sugar. I'm not accusing you of anything. Call Joey, I'll treat you both to lunch."

In less than a half hour they were on the road, Joey squirming with excitement. Amanda had to admit to being a bit excited herself. For the next several hours she'd be with Hawk.

"I want to stop in and talk to an attorney when we're there," Hawk said.

"Why?"

"To add strength to our allegations with Standish. If we have him contact your attorney when requesting his cattle back, he'll know we mean business."

Amanda kept silent for a few minutes. Finally she took a deep breath. "I don't think I can afford an attorney. Not just to negotiate the release of the cattle. If I have a legal battle, then of course I'd have to get one."

He glanced sharply at her. "Money problems?"

She shook her head, gazing straight ahead. "No problems, just it's a bit tight. I have to pay extra to have things delivered from Thermopolis because I live so far away. I don't know what the cattle or horse sales will bring this year, so have to be frugal with what money I have."

Damn. So money was a problem. Hawk opened his mouth to offer to pay the attorney, then snapped it shut. She had too much pride to accept. Thinking about it, they really didn't need one. His brother could advise them on what to say. If it did get into a legal battle, Alec could recommend someone who wouldn't charge an arm and a leg.

"Are we getting ice-cream cones?" Joey asked.

Hawk relaxed. He'd worry about Amanda's money problems another time. He wanted to enjoy today with her, and her son.

"We sure are, right after we eat lunch. Then you'll have to show me around Thermopolis. I've never been there."

"It's a pretty big town," Joey said importantly. "I've been there lots. Right, Mommy?"

"Right, honey. We'll walk around and show Hawk everything there is to see."

The day was perfect as far as Amanda was concerned. Hawk asked Joey where he wanted to eat and cheerfully accepted the Hamburger Haven. When their order was served, Joey mimicked Hawk. He squirted ketchup on his French fries, just like Hawk. He added a pickle to his burger, just like Hawk.

Amanda was amused, and more than once her gaze locked with Hawk's. Amusement wasn't the only emotion she detected. Flushing each time, she'd look away. Only to be drawn again to Hawk's gaze.

"Finished?" he asked, glancing at her basket. There were still a handful of French fries.

"Want to finish my fries?" she asked, pushing the basket across the booth.

"Yep." He reached for them, his fingers brushing against hers. Amanda stilled. His hand caught hers; he laced his fingers with hers and reached for the fries with his left hand. It seemed so intimate. She glanced around, but no one else in the restaurant seemed to notice anything amiss. Gradually she tried to relax.

"How about you, partner, almost finished?" Hawk asked Joey.

"I'm getting full," the little boy responded. He'd eaten most of his child's plate. Only a crescent of burger and roll remained.

"Too full for ice cream?"

"No!"

Hawk smiled and looked back at Amanda. She couldn't believe he could carry on a conversation with Joey. She was totally flustered. Every nerve ending in her body quivered at his touch. Her fingers tingled, the sensation electrifying her arm, her breasts, her stomach. She wondered if he remembered their fingers were entwined. She could scarcely breathe and he acted as if nothing was any different.

"How about you?"

"What about me?" she asked, losing track of the topic.

"Too full for ice cream?" His look darkened, his fingers tightened.

Slowly Amanda shook her head.

"How about something else sweet?" he asked in a soft voice.

"Like what?" Mesmerized by the lights dancing in his eyes, she couldn't look away if the place caught on fire.

"Like one of your kisses?"

Desire flooded. Instantly she knew she wanted one of his hot, demanding, soul-shaking kisses. She wanted to taste his unique flavor, give in to the craving that pounded through her veins, feel again the shimmering waves of pleasure his touch brought.

They were in a public restaurant, but the sight and sounds faded as she imagined the two of them in a tight embrace. Like the one on the porch. Like the one by the fence. Like the ones in her dreams.

"If you keep looking at me like that, I'm likely to forget where we are and drag you across this table," Hawk warned, his eyes hot.

She smiled, and nodded. Was she agreeing to his idea?

"Can we go now?" Joey asked, oblivious to the palatable tension.

"I think it would be a good idea," Hawk said. He squeezed her fingers one last time and released them. Picking up his hat, he slammed it on his head and scooted out of the booth.

Amanda led the way from the Hamburger Haven, conscious of Hawk's eyes on her as she wove her way through the tables. Behind her she could hear Joey's steady stream of conversation, what kind of ice cream he wanted, what kind of cone. But she felt detached, a bit apart. Disoriented. She wished they were back at the Royal Flush. Wished they could find a quiet corner somewhere and give in to the craving to kiss each other.

Once on the sidewalk, Hawk recaptured her hand, holding it against his hard callused palm. He didn't look at her, but gazed around the town's main street.

"Which way to ice cream?" he asked.

"It's across the street. We'll pass a photography store on the way. Maybe they can do one-hour developing."

"Lead on."

Once she got over the shock of a man holding her hand, Amanda decided she liked it. People smiled at them as they passed. Joey ran ahead, darted back to exclaim over what he'd seen. He saw nothing odd about Hawk holding her hand. As Amanda relaxed, her own hand gripped his. Once again she felt special, almost cherished.

It was probably childish, but she didn't care. For the first time in her life she was walking down a street holding a man's hand. She loved it.

They dropped off the film, got their ice-cream cones and wandered along window-shopping. When they came to a pharmacy, Hawk stopped her.

"You and Joey wait here. I need to get something."

He walked inside, glancing over his shoulder to make sure she stayed out front. He headed for the back, and the rack of condoms near the pharmacist's station. He glanced around again, feeling almost as guilty as he had the first time he bought a box as a teenager. He didn't know if he would ever get the chance to use them, but he would not take any chances with Amanda. He wanted her. If she ever grew to feel the same way, he wanted to be able to

protect her. And there was no way he would buy condoms in Tagget. If he believed Standish's cowboy,
the town already suspected he was sleeping with
Amanda; no way would he give them any more fuel
for their malicious gossip.

"What did you buy?" Joey asked when Hawk rejoined them on the sidewalk.

"Just some things. You finished your cone already?"

"Yep. Where are we going now?"

"There's a nice park two blocks over, want go play
on the swings until the film is ready?" Amanda
asked.

"Yes!" Joey started running down the sidewalk
until Hawk called him. He stopped on a dime and
waited for the adults to catch up.

"You stay close," Hawk admonished.

"Okay. Are you going to swing, too, Hawk? I bet
I can go higher than you."

"I think I'm a bit big to swing. But I'll push you.
And your mother, if she wants to swing." .

Amanda shook her head. "Don't you think I'm too
big to swing, too?"

"Nope, you look about sixteen. Still young enough
to enjoy swings."

She felt young enough to enjoy things for a change.
She had Hawk to thank for that. She'd felt so old
before her time for so long. But today everything
seemed bright and carefree and the future looked rosy.
Hawk would get Tom Standish to stop harassing her.
With his help she could get more of the tasks done
around the ranch. And he was so good with Joey.

For a moment she let herself dream they were a
family on an outing. The reality of their situation

dimmed and she gave in to the fantasy of a make-believe happy family. And at the end of the day they would go home and—

And plunge right back into the problems that sometimes threatened to overwhelm her. Hawk worked for her. He wasn't courting her. Standish remained a threat. And she had the hay to arrange to cut, the bills to pay and a decision to make on how many head of cattle to sell.

The pictures were sharp and clear. Hawk had had two sets printed. He took one set and the negatives and handed the second set to Amanda.

"Keep these."

"What are you doing with the negatives?" she asked, tucking the pictures in her purse.

"Safekeeping. We won't have everything in one place."

"You're not expecting a reenactment of the Johnson County wars, but maybe they'll break into my office?" she asked in disbelief.

He shook his head, reclaimed her hand and started back toward the truck. "No. Just safekeeping. Time to get back to the ranch. We've chores to do."

Joey fell asleep shortly after they left Thermopolis, so Hawk and Amanda kept their voices low. Soon they fell silent. She held on to the golden memory of the afternoon. In the future, she'd be able to look back on it as one shining example of a happy day. A perfect afternoon.

"Want me to carry him in?" Hawk asked when they reached the house.

"No, he needs to wake up or he won't sleep at all tonight," she replied, shaking him gently. "I can manage from here."

"Okay."

"Hawk, thanks for this afternoon. Lunch and all." She could hardly thank the man for holding her hand, he would think her certifiable.

"My pleasure. We'll have to do it again sometime. Joey had fun, even before we went to the park. Think about letting him come with me next time I go into Tagget."

She shook her head. "I don't want him there."

"Just think about it, sugar." He climbed out of the car.

"Wait, you forgot your bag." She reached for the plastic bag, catching hold of the wrong end. In two seconds the box of condoms and receipt tumbled out on the floor of the truck. Amanda stared at it. Her eyes flew to Hawk.

Dull red stained his cheeks; his eyes met hers and she could tell he hadn't wanted her to know what he'd bought.

"Just in case," he mumbled, grabbing for the bag, the box and the cash register slip. He spun away and walked toward the bunkhouse, his long stride eating up the distance.

Amanda leaned back against the seat, her son still sleeping against her. *Just in case.* Her heart soared. He still wanted her. He'd done what he could to insure she would be protected. The entire situation was so vastly different from Bobby Jack it amazed her. And she was interested. *Very* interested.

* * *

Being interested and showing that interest were two different things, Amanda discovered as the evening progressed.

She'd watched Hawk during dinner, whenever he wasn't looking her way. Despite the fact she'd known him for such a short time, his features were dearly familiar. She'd like to trace the hard planes of his cheeks, feel the thickness of his hair, mold his muscles with her palms. And she'd like to hear his voice talking low in her ear, saying words meant only for her.

Again and again she remembered the box that had spilled out. And each time she grew warm. But how did she let him know she might be interested in carrying their relationship a step further? In being maybe more than a boss, at least for a little while.

He said good-night after dinner just like Walt and Pepe. The three of them headed for the bunkhouse. She couldn't believe it. Was he planning to come back later, after Joey went to bed?

By the time ten o'clock came around, Amanda knew Hawk was not coming.

She climbed into her bed, the same one she'd had since she moved to the Royal Flush as a teenager. It wasn't very large. Certainly not large enough for a man Hawk's size.

Was she really thinking about making love with a man? For the last six years she'd shunned any overtures. She'd vowed to make her own way, without the entanglement of a man. But that was before she met Hawk.

And before she saw the box of condoms tumble out.

She could do this. She was twenty-three years old.

She had had a handful of dates, made love once. Time she moved on. She was an adult now. She could do this.

As long as she didn't let her heart become involved. She knew Hawk planned to leave when he found a ranch. But until then, she and he could explore the attraction that had flared between them. It wasn't love.

She had thought herself in love with Bobby Jack. And that had proved to be a fleeting emotion at best. Just because she grew tingly inside when Hawk smiled at her didn't mean she was in love. Just because her day seemed brighter when she spent time with him didn't mean anything. The warm glow that spread through her at his compliments didn't mean anything, either. His kindness to her son could melt her heart, but it wasn't love she felt when she watched him with Joey.

Wanting to be with someone every moment of the day, wanting to build a future, wanting to depend on a person, didn't mean she was in love.

Did it?

Oh, God, no! She would not fall for a traveling cowboy. She'd learned her lesson very well. In this case sex and love had nothing to do with each other. She could have sex with Hawk. Love she'd save for Joey.

She curled into a ball, and thought back to her perfect afternoon. Smiling at the memory, she fell asleep.

Amanda was working in her office the next afternoon when Hawk appeared in the doorway. Filled it was more like it, she thought as she put down the pencil and looked up. She felt the tiny kick in her heart and all she could think about was the box of condoms she'd seen.

"What's up?" she asked.

"Just wanted to talk." He ambled in and sat in the chair opposite the desk. Tilting his hat back, he studied her for a moment.

"About what?" she asked warily.

"About what you want to do with the Royal Flush."

"What do you mean?"

"Amanda, the place needs more work than the four of us can do. Your buildings need repair, maintenance to keep them in top shape. There's a leak in the barn, the corral fencing—"

"I know all that needs to be done," she interrupted. She knew more and better than he did. Did he think she was blind?

"Money's tight," he said.

"I'm doing all right."

"All right is not doing well. You need some more men. Can you afford to pay them?"

Frantically she tried to compute figures in her mind. If she hired on another hand, and sold a few more steers, if the hay crop came in as large as last year—

"If you have to think that long about it, I guess you can't."

"I could manage one more," she said defiantly.

"You need three. And one of them should know a hell of a lot more about horses than I do. I'm a cattle man."

"I know a lot about horses."

"But you don't have the time to spend with them.

You've essentially got two operations going here. And I'd guess neither is as successful as it could be.''

"I suppose you think you could do better!"

"Knock the chip off your shoulder, sugar. I think you've done the best you can with all the problems you've encountered. But you won't make it the way you're going." He stared at her. He'd thought about her dilemma long and hard, ever since the ride into town yesterday. His solution wasn't quite what he wanted, but it would do. And it didn't mean someday he couldn't buy a place of his own.

"I could buy into the ranch," he said.

"What?" She stared at him as if he'd just grown a second head. "No."

"A knee-jerk reaction. You haven't even thought about it."

"I don't need to think about it. I'm not selling my ranch."

"I'm not buying your ranch, I'm offering to buy into it. I've got some money. You need money. We'd form a partnership and—"

"No. I'm not getting hooked up with some itinerant cowboy who wandered in a couple of days ago with a few bucks in his pockets. I'm certainly not turning over a portion of my ranch. Did Pembroke put you up to it?"

Hawk felt his temper flare. "Hell, no. I've never met the man."

"Get out, Hawk. I don't need your money or your help."

"You sure as hell need something, sugar. You're going to run this place into the ground if you don't get some money into it." He surged to his feet, wanting to smash something. She was so frustrating. Didn't she realize he wanted to help?

"Don't you worry about me, cowboy. I'll get the money somewhere!" She rose to face him, her fists resting on the desktop.

"If you're waiting for the free ride from the banker's son, he isn't going to deliver!" he roared.

She blinked. Swallowed. The pierce of pain almost blinded her. She dropped her gaze to the desk as she slowly sat back down.

"*Damn!* I didn't mean to say that, Amanda. I swear I didn't mean it." His blasted temper had bested him again. As he watched the color drain from her face, he knew he'd crossed the line. It had been low-down and cruel. And he really didn't mean it. She'd been an infatuated kid. She was a mature adult now.

"I think you'd better leave, Hawk."

"Amanda, I didn't mean that."

She nodded, her eyes blank. The hurt was unbearable. She had no one to blame but herself. She shouldn't have hired him. Shouldn't have told him her background. She should have kept him at a distance, like Walt or Pepe.

"Amanda—"

"Please go."

He looked at her for a long moment, then turned and strode quickly from the room. Walking quickly down the hall, he slammed his fist against the wall. Damnation! His foul temper had really done it now. He'd hurt her when he had wanted to help her. When was he going to learn to control it? To think before acting, to consider his words before hurling them?

Hawk paused on the top step, gazing over the yard toward the barn. He hadn't meant to hurt her, and now he didn't have a clue how to make her feel better. He'd practically accused her of being a whore. She wouldn't take it lightly. How could he make amends?

And he wanted to. He'd only known her for a few days, but he found he liked her smile, liked the way her eyes lit up and became all silvery when she was happy. He wanted to see her that way again, not the cold, lifeless woman he'd just left.

Damn!

"Hi, Hawk. Can we go riding again?" Joey called to him from the corral.

Slowly Hawk walked toward the boy. At least he was able to make one of the Williamses happy.

Amanda took a shaky breath, absently rubbing the pain in her chest. She dashed away the tears that had somehow leaked from her eyes. She had been called worse. There was nothing to get so upset about. Certainly not from some two-bit cowboy who meant nothing to her.

That was a lie. He meant more than he should to her. Dammit. She had thought she was in charge of her emotions, but his awful comment made her aware of how much she'd grown to like him over the past few days. How much she had wanted his approval, his companionship. And all the time he was scoping out her place with an intent to purchase.

Had he expected her to be so grateful she'd sell half her inheritance? It was the only thing she had of her own, and she would hold on to it for all she was worth. It enabled her to earn a living, keep Joey safe and do something she loved. She would never jeopardize it. Not for a man who thought she had tried to gain an easy life by sleeping with the town's rich boy.

She drew the checkbook to the center of the desk and quickly wrote a check to Hawk for the days worked. Tearing it from the book, she felt a pang. For a few days she'd thought she'd found someone to be comfortable with. She remembered their afternoon—was it just yesterday?

Foolish dreams from a foolish girl. She wasn't some teenager holding hands with a dream date. She was a grown woman with a ranch to run and a son to raise.

She found Hawk in the barn currying one of the horses. Joey worked with him, brushing the forelegs of the gelding and jabbering away.

"Joey." She paused a couple of feet away. "Joey, honey, go into the house and get yourself some lemonade."

"Aw, Mommy, I'm helping Hawk with Geronimo. I'm brushing his legs."

"The horse will be here when you get back. Go on."

She refused to look at Hawk, though she knew he'd stopped his work and watched her. Joey put the brush on the bench and walked slowly from the barn.

Amanda held out the check. "I believe this covers the days you've worked here."

Hawk didn't move a muscle.

"As soon as Pepe or Walt comes in, one of them can drive you into town." Her hand didn't shake, her voice was calm. Nothing betrayed the agonizing turmoil that plagued her. She refused to remember her dreams. Life wasn't comprised of dreams. Surely she'd already learned that.

"I'm not leaving," he said at last.

Her eyes met his, and she straightened, standing

even taller. "You're fired," she stated clearly. "I want you off my ranch as soon as one of the others can drive you."

He tossed the brush at the bench and stepped closer, careful not to crowd her, not to touch her.

"I'm not leaving, Amanda. I'm sorry as hell for what I said. I didn't mean it even as I said it. I know I have the devil's own temper and it gets me in more trouble than it should. But I'm not going. Be mad at me, yell and scream, throw a fit. Don't speak to me for a week. But then forgive me, sugar. I'm most damnably sorry."

"I'm not your sugar." On that her voice did break, just a little. "And I want you off the ranch. There's nothing for you here."

"I'm starting to think you're wrong on that. I think there's a lot here for both of us, if we just see where it'll lead us."

With that, he took a step closer and pressed his lips against hers, drawing her into his arms. She was stiff, but he didn't care. He only wanted to hold her, feel her soft feminine body against his, breathe in the scent of her, taste her honey sweetness once more. He may have ruined things forever, but he dare not believe it. He wanted her. And nothing he'd said or done had changed that.

But did she still have any interest in him? Or had he crushed any possibility? He'd have to use all his persuasive powers to find out.

Seven

Oh, how she had wanted his kiss. But not like this. Not with the hateful words still echoing in her mind. Her arms and hands were trapped between them. She should push him away, slap his face, order him from the ranch instantly. But she couldn't resist just one more second of his embrace.

His mouth pressed against hers, moving persuasively, provocatively. His hands held her immobile. She could feel his strength, his heat. Heady with reaction, she felt her legs grow weak. Clutching his shirt, she knew she had to step back, end this delight. It wasn't fair. She wanted to bask in his touch, delight in being with him. Draw from his strength.

But he proved to be no different from the men in town. No different from the people she'd been fighting for six years. Better to find out now than after she'd made an irrevocable mistake.

His lips moved to her cheek, kissing her gently. He moved to her ear, kissing the lobe.

"You can yell and scream, kick my shins, not talk to me for a week, but let me stay, Amanda. Let me stay," he said softly, still hugging her tightly, his breath warm against her ear.

She shivered, closing her eyes as indecision raked her. He had to leave. She couldn't let him stay after what he'd said. Yet being held felt so good, seemed so right. She had to pull back, had to end the madness, but not for another second. Just one more second of feeling cherished before she'd send him away.

"Amanda." The urgency in his voice penetrated and she pushed against his chest. He moved his head to rest his forehead on hers, gazing deep into her eyes.

The tears he saw almost pierced his heart. He had never felt such pain. Not after a fight, not after bronc riding. To know he'd caused such anguish to the woman he admired hurt more than anything.

"You need me to stay, Amanda. You need the work I can do. Don't let my temper ruin this. Please."

She blinked, holding back the tears. His heart twisted at the effort she expended. Slowly, he closed his eyes and sought her mouth again. She responded. God, he wanted her more than ever. And he knew he'd be lucky if she ever spoke to him again.

Damn his temper!

Walt and Pepe rode in together. Hawk heard them coming and released Amanda, stepping back toward the gelding he had been brushing.

She faced away from the barn door and brushed her fingertips across her cheeks. Without another word to Hawk, she turned and left. He watched her go, an unsatisfactory relief hitting. She still had the check. She hadn't said he could stay, but she hadn't ordered him to leave again. And she had kept the check.

It would be enough for now.

Amanda nodded to Pepe and Walt and walked swiftly to the house. Her mouth still felt the impression of Hawk's, her back could still feel the warmth of his arms and hands. Her heart still raced out of control. And he was still on the ranch. Damn him.

"Hi, Mommy." Joey sat at the table, carefully finishing a glass of lemonade. "I'm done, can I go help Hawk again?"

She hesitated, wanting to snatch up her little boy and hide him away from Hawk's influence. She didn't like Joey becoming so attached to the man. As soon as she could afford to hire another hand, she'd make sure Hawk left and never came back. She should shelter her son from the future.

But Hawk was here now and Joey loved being with him. Sighing regretfully, she nodded. "Sure, just don't be a pest."

"I'm not. He likes me to help." He scrambled off the chair and raced from the kitchen.

Amanda continued into the office. Walking to the desk, she glanced down. She still held the check. His final check. Staring at it for a long moment, she shook her head and crumbled it into her fist. Pitching it into the trash, she sat down behind the desk and pulled the books close. She had to find the money to hire more men. At least one additional—and one to replace Hawk. Maybe if she advertised in the Cheyenne paper she'd get results.

* * *

Amanda caught Joey at one point late in the afternoon and sent him to find Walt.

"Hey, Amanda, you wanted to see me?" Walt stood in the doorway, his hat turning around and around in his hands.

"I do. Come in and sit for a minute." She took a breath. "I want you to act as foreman for the Royal Flush."

"What?" The old man looked startled.

"I want to work more with the horses, and I need someone to ramrod the cattle side of it. You were here with Jonas for years. You've probably forgotten more than I'll ever learn. I've placed an ad in the Cheyenne paper for more men, so you'll have more hands to work with."

He shook his head. "Amanda, I don't know about being a foreman. I've been a cowhand all my life. I've never bossed anyone."

"You just see what needs to be done and tell the men to do it."

"No, honey, I'm not the one to do it. You should put Hawk in charge. He's sharp, hardworking, and he knows plenty about cattle."

"No!" She took a deep breath. "No, I don't think Hawk is the right man. He's leaving soon."

"When he finds a spread. But appears to me he's not looking too hard. He'll be here awhile yet," Walt said sagely.

"I want you, Walt. We can go over things together for the first few days if you like. Until you're comfortable with the situation. Decide together what needs to be done and who's best to do it. Please, Walt." She swallowed hard. She didn't want to have to beg him to take the job, but she was growing desperate. She didn't want to deal with Hawk Blackstone again.

"Sure, if that's what you want, honey. What'll I do first?"

She relaxed marginally, the first step behind her.

They discussed the most important tasks for the next week, who would best suit which one. Amanda took notes as they talked, handing them to Walt at the end of the discussion.

"Here, this is what we decided. Now you know just what to have Pepe and Hawk do. If something comes up, use your best judgment."

"You leaving?" he asked suddenly.

"No, of course not. Only, I'm going to spend more time with the horses. I made a bit on the last sale. I want to devote more time to them, see if I can improve the strains, build up that side of the ranch."

"Yeah, you always were horse crazy. Okay, Amanda, I'll do my best."

She smiled warmly, feeling safe for the first time that afternoon. "I know you will, Walt, thanks."

Amanda cooked fried chicken for dinner. She made mounds of mashed potatoes, heated green beans and baked biscuits. Cooking soothed her. She had always liked it, from the first day she'd come to live with Jonas. For the first time in her life she had felt needed, an important member of a team.

She missed Jonas, still had trouble some days believing that she'd never see him again. He had been gruff and strict, but loving in his own way. She wished her mother had returned some of his feelings. Maybe he could have become her stepfather. Though she couldn't have loved him any more than she already had.

Once everyone was seated and the dinner served, Amanda cleared her throat.

All eyes turned to her.

"I wanted to let you know that I made Walt foreman today. He'll be in charge from now on. I've placed an ad in the Cheyenne paper for some more men. Walt will help me in the hiring process." She looked at Pepe as she talked, refusing to meet Hawk's eyes, though she could feel them burning into her.

"It's a small spread to need a foreman," Pepe commented.

"I'm not going to work on the cattle side anymore. I'm going to work with my horses." She refused to look at Hawk.

"Well, congratulations, old friend. You're coming up in the world," Pepe said with a broad smile at his longtime crony.

"Yeah, well, it wasn't my idea," Walt grumbled.

Amanda looked down at her dinner, her appetite gone. Could she excuse herself and leave? Or would—

The sound of a vehicle in the yard caught her attention. She rose and crossed to the door, curious. They rarely had visitors. Her heart dropped when she saw who had pulled up. Sheriff Yates and Tom Standish climbed out of the sheriff's black-and-white car.

"Who's here, Mommy?" Joey asked, about to get down from his chair.

"Eat your dinner, Joey. It's Tom Standish and the sheriff."

Hawk rose and crossed the room in two long strides to stand beside her. She didn't look at him, but some of her unease faded.

"Amanda." Sheriff Yates nodded to her when he stood on the other side of the screen door.

"Sheriff. What brings you out here?"

"Business. Need to talk to you."

"Come in." She pushed open the door and turned, almost bumping into Hawk. "We were in the middle of dinner," she said as she sidestepped around Hawk and headed for the office.

"I hope this won't take long," Sheriff Yates said as he and Tom followed her down the hall into her office. Hawk brought up the rear, the heels of his boots sounding loud on the wooden floor.

Despite everything, she appreciated his standing with her. She didn't want to stand alone.

"You know Tom," the sheriff said.

Amanda nodded. "But Hawk doesn't. Hawk Blackstone, this is Tom Standish, and Sheriff Parker Yates."

Tom studied the cowboy for a long moment, his eyes narrowed. Then he swung around to look at Amanda. He remained silent, glaring at her.

"Amanda, Tom's brought a charge of rustling against you," Sheriff Yates began.

"Rustling! Are you crazy? I would never rustle any cattle," she exclaimed.

Hawk's anger began to build, even as he admired the tactic. Tom Standish was not an easy antagonist.

"He says you've got some of his cattle," the sheriff said.

"I didn't rustle them. Good heavens, you know I would never do such a thing."

"Of course he does," Hawk said easily, only his fists betraying the adrenaline pumping through him, the flickering tendrils of anger that pulsed. "It's a bluff, sugar. But you've got to admire his nerve."

"It's no bluff. Amanda stole over forty head of my cattle, mingled them with her own cattle. They're grazing right now on her land."

"How do you know that?" Hawk asked.

Tom stared at him. The sheriff spun around, looking between Hawk and Tom, picking up the vibrations.

"What do you mean?" Tom asked. For the first time since entering the house, a hint of unease crossed his face.

"How do you know how many head are on Amanda's land? And why do you think she stole them?" Hawk said patiently, his attention focused on the rancher.

"I'm missing that many head and who else would take them?"

"Nobody took them—they were driven over by your own cowboys. Not for the first time, either," Amanda spoke up.

"That's a lie."

"Only this time," Hawk continued as if Tom had not spoken, "we didn't return them. I posted a sign in town about grazing fees. Seems to me you owe Amanda a sizable chunk of change."

"This is preposterous! Sheriff, I demand you arrest Amanda for rustling. Arrest all of them, they're probably all in it together."

"Now, Tom, hold on here. We need to make sure of our facts before we go arresting anyone," Sheriff Yates said, looking between Tom and Hawk.

"Bring out the pictures, sugar," Hawk said softly, his eyes never leaving Tom's.

"What pictures?" the sheriff asked.

"He's got a picture or two of Matt and Jeremy near some cut fence," Tom said dismissively. "It's a plant. This cowhand probably cut the wire and then lured my men over to take a picture."

Amanda handed the stack of pictures to Sheriff Yates. "This is not the first time, either," she said. "Since Jonas died, I've repaired that stretch of fence at least seven times. And every other time I found cattle grazing on my land, I herded them back. Except this time. Now I'm charging for use of my grazing land."

"You better look at these, Tom." The sheriff handed the pictures to the rancher.

"We've also got three witness who will testify that Standish's men cut the fence," Hawk said softly. "Up against such irrefutable evidence, do you think these cowboys are going to deny doing it, or admit they were following boss's orders?"

Tom threw the photos onto the desk, glaring at Amanda. "You win this round. I'll send my boys for my cattle."

"Once you've paid the grazing fee," she said, standing tall, meeting his gaze with a hard one of her own. "I'm tired of being pushed around, Tom. I never did anything to you. Jonas left me the ranch, and I'm not selling. Keep your cowboys away from the fence and keep your cattle on your own land."

"Now see here, you little sl—"

"I'd ride easy with the words, mister." Hawk stepped closer. He topped Tom by three inches, his shoulders were broader, he was at least twenty years younger. And his stance let Tom know exactly what would happen if he said a single word Hawk didn't like.

"Standish, I'd advise you to pay the lady, get your cattle and stay the hell away from the Royal Flush in the future," Sheriff Yates said. With a disgruntled snort, he strode from the room.

Tom hesitated, then turned to follow the sheriff. "I'll send a check tomorrow when my men come for the cattle," He spit out the words.

Amanda didn't move. She held her breath as she listened to the two men walk through the house. She heard the screen door slam, the sound of the sheriff's car starting and pulling away.

Her gaze flickered toward Hawk, then away. "Thank you," she said. If it hadn't been for him she shuddered to think how the interview might have gone. If she had not had the photographs, would the sheriff have believed her, or Tom?

Had this ended her problems with Standish, or only moved them to another plane? Time would tell. For tonight, she had won this skirmish. Maybe there wouldn't be a war, after all.

"Sure thing, sugar. You did good yourself."

His praise warmed her more than it should have. She nodded and indicated the door. "Dinner is getting cold."

"After you," he said, waiting.

She shook her head. She refused to get that close to Hawk again. "I want to be alone for a few minutes. I'll be there directly."

When he'd gone, she sat down in her chair, giving way to the shaky knees that had plagued her during the entire confrontation. She'd done it. Not alone, of course, but the triumph proved sweet, nonetheless.

She'd bested Tom Standish. And the sheriff had stood up for her. That astonished her more than anything.

Yet she owed it all to Hawk Blackstone. The ache in her heart reminded her of their altercation that afternoon. Nothing had changed because of this. She felt a mixture of gratitude, disappointment and utter desolation. Feeling drained, she leaned back against the chair and closed her eyes.

Hawk tightened the cinch on the horse, pulling it up in a sharp jerk, frustration spilling over. Damn! He'd told her a week ago to not talk to him, but he hadn't meant it. And he hadn't thought she'd do it. He could have taken her screaming. He wished she had vented her anger and hurt by any other means.

It had been six days since he last spoke to Amanda, except at meals. Then she refused to look at him, or speak to him, unless he gave her no choice. Walt handed out assignments each morning like some marine sergeant, even referring to some written notes on paper to do so. And he made sure Hawk got the assignments farthest from the house.

"As if I didn't know whose dumb idea that was," Hawk mumbled, pulling down the stirrup and checking the saddle one more time. Swinging up, he pulled his hat low on his forehead and kicked the horse. In seconds they were flying across the open range, away from the house, headed for another day of checking the fencing on the far perimeter.

"One day you're going to have to forgive me," he muttered as the wind whipped by, the sun sparkling in the clear sky. It would be another warm day. Another quiet, lonely day riding by himself, thinking of Amanda.

He wanted her every time he saw her. Sometimes in the morning she'd fix breakfast with her hair tied back, her cheek still creased with a sheet imprint. It was all he could do to resist taking her face in his hands and kissing her.

Only the evenings were worse. She'd be flushed and rosy from cooking, smell of the wonderful aromas of bread and flowers and her own unique scent. He'd want to gather her close and hold her, just hold her.

Well, maybe a bit more.

A whole lot more.

Tightening his hand on the reins, he tried to outrun his thoughts. But they kept pace. She was slowly driving him crazy. The only thing that kept him around was the strong feeling he wasn't alone in this. He never caught her looking at him, but sensed she studied him when he wasn't looking at her. He knew she listened to him at dinner, even while pretending to ignore him.

And he had not imagined her response to his kisses. He wanted her and he suspected she wanted him.

And hated the fact.

Damnation! Why hadn't he learned control of his temper yet?

It was riding him now. He was so angry at the time wasted, at the impenetrable wall she'd erected, he could spit nails. Maybe the time had come to change things. He wasn't sure they could get worse.

Amanda left the tack room and crossed the barn when she heard the trucks pull into the yard, wondering who had come today. Tom had sent a check with the four men sent to retrieve his cattle the day after their confrontation. She was still astonished at the amount. It was accurate, seven dollars a day for forty head of cattle, for all the days they'd been on her range.

She stopped near the opening, suddenly wary. None of the men were around. Hawk had been sent to the far range, Walt was working near the river and Pepe had gone into town. Two pickup trucks pulled to a halt. The same two men who had cut her fence climbed out. Taking a deep breath, she wondered what they wanted.

"Ms. Williams." Matt slammed the door of his truck and tipped his hat. In only a minute his partner climbed out of his truck and came to stand beside him.

"What can I do for you?" she asked. They kept their distance. Surely they wouldn't try anything. They had no way of knowing she was here alone.

"Actually, ma'am, I came by to apologize to you. I didn't realize you were nearby when I said some things at the fence that day. I'm sorry you had to hear it. I was repeating things I'd heard in town." He rubbed his palms on his jeans nervously and glanced at his partner. "I...that is Jeremy and I are sorry about cutting the fence. I knew it was wrong, but I followed orders," Matt said, uncomfortably.

"The matter has been resolved," she said stiffly.

"Yes, ma'am." He stood there, glancing around the place. The man at his side studied the ground in front of him.

"Was there something else?" Amanda asked.

Matt cleared his throat, glanced again at his partner, then back at Amanda. "Actually, there is, ma'am. We heard, that is we were wondering, I mean someone said you might have a couple of openings on the Royal Flush.''

Startled, she froze for a moment. The last thing she needed was to hire some cowboy who thought she slept around. She'd heard every word he'd said that day by the draw. That attitude was hard enough to take in town, she didn't need to bring it to the Royal Flush.

Matt cleared his throat. "If you do, we'd like to apply. I know we didn't start off too good, ma'am, but if you could overlook that. We were following orders. We're good at that,'' he said earnestly.

"He fired us," Jeremy said bluntly, his eyes meeting Amanda's. "Said he didn't need incompetents who didn't know any better than to be caught out by a woman.''

She looked away, almost wanting to smile at the parroting of Tom Standish's words. She could use the help. She had heard nothing on the ad in the Cheyenne paper. Yet she couldn't help but remember what Matt had suggested. Weighing everything, she tried to come up with the right decision. Maybe she could give them a try. It wasn't as if they could do anything to her while she had the other cowboys around. And she sure did need more help around the ranch. Tom's check would more than cover their salary for a month or so until she could sell some cattle. She smiled. Wouldn't he have a fit if he knew?

"I might be willing to give you a try. Shall we go into the office and discuss terms?''

"Yes, ma'am!''

Amanda was uncertain with her decision as she sat at the dinner table that evening. Walt hadn't been enthusiastic about hiring the two men. He hadn't forgotten their involvement in the fence cutting. But she had assured him she thought they would work out. Or was it wishful thinking on her part?

She had been more nervous about Hawk's reaction. But he had said nothing, talking easily with the men, catching them up with information they'd need to do their job.

When they talked, she studied each of them. Matt and Jeremy weren't much younger than Hawk, yet they seemed boys compared to him. Some of it was due to their constant teasing of each other, and Joey. But there was something else. Some intangible thing that put Hawk a bit ahead of them in maturity. She couldn't define it, but she recognized it.

It was obvious Matt and Jeremy had been friends for a long time. They shared the same kind of humor, same carefree outlook on life. And they were as comfortable with each other as Pepe and Walt.

Amanda watched them warily during dinner, but they never mentioned anything that could be taken the wrong way. And the two new cowboys kept everyone on their toes. Joey was enchanted with their banter. He laughed, and tried his hand at teasing back.

Amanda wondered if he would change his allegiance to these new men, pulling back a bit from Hawk. It wouldn't hurt to have other younger men on the place. Give the boy several role models.

But Joey still hung on Hawk's every word. Still checked with Hawk if he was uncertain about something. A week ago she would have liked that. Now she found it unsettling. Joey shouldn't get too attached to the man. He'd be moving on soon.

In fact, she could let him go now. The two new hands easily replaced Hawk.

Suddenly the idea lost its appeal. Maybe she'd wait just a few days longer, to see how things worked out. Maybe Walt was right and the two new men wouldn't do a good job for them. She didn't need to rush into firing Hawk.

Not that she thought she could. Hadn't she tried that a week ago? He flat out had not listened. Had kissed her senseless instead.

Heat stole into her cheeks and she gazed firmly on her plate, lest anyone guess her thoughts. If she tried to fire him again, would he kiss her again?

"Can I ride with Hawk, Mommy?" Joey asked excitedly. "Can I?"

"What?" She looked up. She had missed the conversation, too deep in thought. "What?"

"Can I ride with Hawk tomorrow?"

Involuntarily she glanced at the man. His gaze caught hers. It was the first time she'd looked into his eyes since that day. The dark blue seemed deeper than before. And she could discern a trace of lingering hurt. Suddenly, realization dawned—*he hurt because he'd hurt her!*

Catching her breath, she tried to look away but couldn't. Helplessly gazing deep into the stormy depth of Hawk's eyes, she felt herself yearning to make things right between them. To recapture the easy friendship they'd been forging when he'd said the unforgivable words.

She knew it was dangerous. Knew it could lead to more heartache. But, oh, how she longed for the delight in his company, the sense of right and belonging that she found around him.

"Yes, Joey, you can ride with Hawk tomorrow," she said, dragging her gaze away. Glancing around the table she was relieved to see none of the others noticed anything amiss. None saw the rapid beat of her heart. None saw the craving for Hawk that saturated her being.

She longed to escape but she remained. Every cell attuned to Hawk, it was the most difficult dinner she'd sat through. Every second seemed like an hour. Conscious of the man sitting mere inches away, it took all her self-control to finish her meal, to calmly talk to the others as if it were a normal day. To laugh at the jokes, and give back the teasing. She was exhausted by the time the meal ended.

Grateful for the dishes and other chores before bed, Amanda watched the men file out, Joey following.

"Be back by eight-thirty," she admonished her son.

Once she had put Joey to bed, Amanda wandered out to the porch and sank onto the swing. Pushing to and fro, she gazed over her ranch. There was so much she wanted to accomplish, so much to do to make it profitable, and successful. Sometimes she wondered if she were up to it. She didn't have all the knowledge that she needed. Sometimes she didn't have the energy. Maybe with Walt sharing some of the burden, things would prove easier. Maybe she could recapture her joy in the ranch.

"Amanda?"

She turned. Hawk stood on the bottom step. Her heart caught in her throat.

"Hawk," she acknowledged.

He tucked his hands into the front pockets of his

jeans, trying to see her clearly in the faint light. "We need to talk," he said slowly.

"About what?" Her nerves were still raw from dinner.

"About my staying."

Amanda stopped the swing, stood and walked closer. "What about it?"

"You needed me before. Now you have two more hands. Do you want me to go or stay?"

She rubbed her damp palms against her jeans. She didn't need this. "What do you want to do?"

"Doesn't matter. This is your place, you make the calls. What is it you want, Amanda? Shall I stay, or pack up and leave in the morning? It's your decision. I stayed after...after the other day because I knew you needed me. Matt and Jeremy's coming changes that. I can stay and work for you awhile longer, or leave. Which is it?"

She didn't want to decide something like that. He'd taken the decision from her last week. Why was he bringing it up now? Did he know what an awkward position he put her in? Did he care? She should send him away. He'd hurt her unbearably. But why? It was no more than most of the people in Tagget thought.

If she told him to go, he'd leave. She knew it this time. Knew he'd ride into town, leave Tagget and never look back. She hated the thought of never seeing him again. Never watching his smile, never feeling his strength. She couldn't do that, at least not yet.

Because she had come to care for him, care for his opinion; when he hadn't believed in her, he had shattered her. Or had he only dented her heart? The pain had faded over the past week. A lingering sadness had survived, but nothing earth-shattering. And she missed him. Missed—

"Well, what's it to be? Do I go or stay?"

She hesitated. "Stay, please," she said finally.

"Why?"

"Because I want you to for the sake of the ranch." He'd be moving on soon enough, once the real estate agent found him a ranch of his own. In the meantime, she needed his strength, his knowledge, his presence.

"Stay until you find your ranch," she said, hoping she wasn't making a mistake. Believing she was not.

Eight

"I want you, too," he said, stepping closer.

"What?"

"I want to stay. But I don't want to stay like we have been this week, not speaking, not touching, not sharing thoughts and time together. I want to go back to the way we were the afternoon we spent in Thermopolis. I want you to look at me and talk to me."

He took a step closer.

"I want you to let me kiss you again."

"Just kiss me?" she asked softly, reaching out to touch him. Her hand rested on his chest, she could feel the rapid beat of his heart. She didn't care what the people in town gossiped about. She didn't care about her reputation. She knew who she was.

And she knew the feelings she held for Bobby Jack had been nothing but childish infatuation, a crush on the first good-looking boy who had paid her any at-

tention. Her feelings for this man were vastly different. Deeper, mature, lasting. She hadn't liked the rift
between them. She longed for that awareness that
filled her when near him. Longed to touch him, have
him touch her.

"You know I want more. You know I'm prepared
for more."

She blinked. He referred to the box he'd bought in
Thermopolis. Nodding, she said softly, "I guess I
do."

His hand covered hers, holding it against his hard
chest. "So how do I stay?" he repeated.

"With me?" she asked, stepping closer this time,
until she almost touched him from shoulder to thigh.

"Are you sure, Amanda? I want you to be damned
sure, sugar." His hand came up and brushed against
the side of her face, his fingers moving to her hair.

"I am," she replied even as his face came down
to hers, as his lips covered her mouth and kissed her
long and deep.

His arms came around her and he picked her up.
Carrying her to the swing, he sat down with her in
his lap. His mouth moved against hers, sipping kisses,
taking long deep ones, until Amanda didn't know
which end was up, where she was or that there was
another world surrounding them. Lost in the blissful
sensations that pulsed through her, her hands threaded
through his thick hair, knocking off his hat, reveling
in the feel of him beneath them. She sought to get
even closer, pressing against him as if struggling to
meld with him.

When his lips moved to her jaw, skimmed down
her throat and caressed her, she sighed in delight, wiggling even closer.

"Easy, sugar, we've time enough," he said softly. Slowly he slipped open the top button of her shirt, then the second. Widening the opening with his hands, he lowered his mouth to the tantalizing expanse of skin. He licked her collarbone, kissed it, moved back up her throat and to her waiting lips. She shivered and burned at the same time. Amazing, she thought, when she could.

Trailing her hands down his neck, she molded the strong muscles in his shoulders, slipped down to trace the shape of his hard chest. Heat engulfed her. Desire raged almost out of control.

"Hawk," she said softly, "Please, Hawk, let's go inside."

He stilled, his hands moving to hug her, pull her tightly against him as he tried to get his breathing under control.

"And do what?"

"Make love."

"Are you sure, Amanda? Very, very sure?"

She nodded, afraid, excited, but very, very certain. She loved this man, wanted to share all aspects of love with him. Even if he didn't care the same for her, she would have one glorious night to remember.

He cupped her face in his hard palms and held her back to gaze down into her eyes. The faint light from the moon and stars enabled him to see the expression on her face. She looked well kissed, and happy. His heart flipped. She also looked vulnerable as hell.

He had no intention of hurting her. He only wanted to be with her, to assuage this burning need they both felt around each other. God, she was so beautiful. And she wanted him.

He smiled and dropped a light kiss on her mouth,

his hands already moving to the back of her head, fumbling with the band that held her hair, snapping it and letting her hair flow freely down her back. He drew his fingers through the silken mass, its softness unbelievable. He'd longed to do this since he'd first seen her in the diner. He wanted to see it spilled over a pillow, feel it brush against his chest, keep his hands tangled in it forever.

"Please?" she whispered once again.

"Whatever you want, Amanda. I want you too much to deny either of us."

He stood, carrying her easily, and headed for her room.

"I can walk." But she made no move to be released.

"I know, I've seen you, and a sexy walk it is," he said, dropping another kiss on her pretty mouth. How often had he watched her moving around, and wanted her all the more each time?

"Wait." She pulled back a bit. "Put me down. Hawk, we can't use my room."

He set her on her feet, keeping one arm around her waist. "Why not, too close to Joey's?"

She shook her head. "I only have a single bed."

"So?"

She looked up at him in the darkness of the hallway. She wished she could see him clearly. No, she didn't. It was better to have everything softened by the night. She would never have the nerve to go through with this in broad daylight.

"So we'd be crowded."

"Sounds good to me." He nudged her along, pushing her, kissing her neck, running his hands over her hips, up to her breasts the entire time they moved slowly until they were inside her room.

Closing the door, he asked, "Does it have a lock?"

"No."

"Does Joey tend to get up in the night?"

"Are you kidding? He sleeps like a log." She grew nervous, afraid. Uncertainty rose. Could she do this? She wanted him so much, but could she—

"Hey, sugar, none of that." His mouth found hers, kissed her gently. "I can almost feel the questions and doubts rising. I won't hurt you, Amanda. Never again. I just want to give you pleasure." His hands were brushing through her hair, moving down her back to cup her hips, pulling her in close to him, so she knew exactly how much he wanted her.

Amanda sighed and relaxed against him. The fiery heat would not be kept at bay, and she plunged right in.

By the time they had shucked their clothes—and Hawk had tossed a handful of foil packets on the table and they had fallen into her narrow bed—Amanda was a mass of burning need. She moved her hands over his chest, rubbing against the strong muscles, relishing the tickling sensation of hair. Exploring the skin over his ribs, she traced each one, moving down to sweep across his narrow hips, his hard flanks.

His hand caught hers, brought it around to touch him at his most vulnerable point. Sighing with delightful discovery, she closed around him gently, feeling the heat, the steel, the pulsing desire.

Hawk tried to slow their pace. He wanted to savor every minute with this woman. She was like a wild thing with him, enchanting him with her eagerness to learn, to explore, to feel. He didn't want to end it too

soon, but his own control was slipping. She drove him
crazy, had since day one.

Reaching for one of the foil packets, he readied
himself for her.

"Hawk?"

"Ready, sugar?" He opened her legs, spread them
wide and drew his fingers gently against the heat he
found between them. She was wet and hot and sweet
and he was going crazy with craving.

"Yes." Her arms drew him closer, pulling him
over onto her as she tilted her hips and waited. For
only a second. Then he slid into her, stretching her
and filling her and pleasing her.

"Yes." Amanda breathed again, closing her eyes
to better enjoy the exquisite pleasure that built higher
and higher every time Hawk thrust inside her, every
time his hands caressed her, teaching her the wondrous capability of her own body.

"Hawk, Hawk, Hawk," she chanted his name as
they tumbled over the edge of bliss together. Clinging
to him as if he were her lifeline, she gave in to the
ecstasy he built. The pleasure pulsed through her entire body, endlessly. Time stopped and only sensation
and delight had any meaning. That and the man who
held her, who kissed her so deeply and raised her so
high.

She had never felt anything like it before. She had
never known her own body could explode with such
pleasure. Slowly, ever so slowly, she regained an
awareness of where she was, who was with her.
Slowly her body settled down, still spasming around
him. Her arms never left him. She wanted him to stay
exactly where he lay forever.

Hawk kissed her jaw, her cheek, her eyes. He laid

his cheek against hers and whispered in her ear, "You okay?"

"Okay is rather mundane, don't you think?" she replied sleepily. "Glorious, stupendous, marvelous, fantastic, maybe. But I don't think okay is the right word."

He chuckled, blew in her ear. "Yeah, well, I think you're right." He kissed his way back to her mouth and pressed his lips against hers gently.

"I'm heavy." He rose up on his arms.

"No, don't go." She tried to draw him closer, but he pulled away.

"I'm not going anywhere, just getting off you before I squish you flat. Oops." He scrambled madly to keep from falling from the bed. A quick lunge for the headboard saved an ignominious fall.

Amanda giggled and scooted to the edge of the narrow bed. "I told you it was small."

"All the better to cuddle closer. I'll be right back." He left the room and Amanda heard him in the bathroom. In only a moment he'd returned.

He lay down beside her, drawing her tightly against him. "There are advantages to a small bed. I like this." One arm lay beneath her head, the other encircled her waist, holding her along his hot naked body.

She relaxed against him, snuggled just a bit, her legs tangled with his. Turning her head, she found him right there. For a moment she wished the light had been on so she could see him. But there was enough light from the nighttime sky to make out his features. Everything looked silvery in the moonlight. He stared at her, his expression grave and serious.

"No regrets?" he asked.

She shook her head, her eyes locking with his. "It

was wonderful. The best time I ever had. And I don't care if the whole world knows it.''

He gave a grin. ''Well, I don't think we need to take an ad out in the local paper. But I'm glad you're not sorry. Go to sleep now.''

''Are you leaving?'' she asked, her hand running down his arm. She loved touching him. Felt so close to him. It was odd, she'd never felt this closeness with anyone before. And she dare not tell him how she felt. He was here until his real estate agent found a ranch for him. He had made her no promises, no commitment. She was not so foolish as to think one night together would change his mind. She knew how men thought, what they wanted.

But for once, she wanted the same thing. Maybe she'd feel differently in the morning, but tonight everything felt just right. She'd made love with the man she loved. And she was happy, truly happy, for the first time in years.

''I'm not going anywhere, sugar. Go to sleep.'' He reached down and drew the sheet and blanket over them.

Closing her eyes, she felt the lassitude sweep through her. She was tired, exhausted and so replete she almost didn't recognize herself. With a smile on her face, she drifted to sleep. Secure in Hawk's arms.

''Amanda?'' Hawk kissed her again. Warm and sweet with sleep, he hated to wake her. But he didn't want to sneak away like a thief. ''Sugar, I'm going now.'' He kissed her again. He'd already dressed. Otherwise he'd probably climb right back in that small bed and love her all over again.

''Hum?''

"I'm going now, before Joey wakes up. I'll see you at breakfast." He kissed her again.

Sleepily she blinked up at him, her mouth smiling when she awoke enough to recognize him. "I wish you didn't have to go," she murmured.

"But I do. Dammit, I don't want to." He kissed her again, his hand cupping her cheek, her jaw. Beneath the blanket she was buck naked, and the thought of seeing her again, this time in the daylight, was almost too tempting to resist. But it would start something they didn't have time for, not this morning. Maybe he could get Walt or Pepe to take the boy one night, make an adventure of staying in the bunkhouse.

Right. That would go a long way to keeping her reputation intact. Maybe he should just take an ad in the local paper.

He stood, ran his fingers through his hair. "I'll see you at breakfast."

"Okay. I'll be getting up now, too," she said, watching him with hungry eyes. He'd made love to her a second time during the night. She was tired, a little sore and glowing. As he left her room, Amanda sighed softly and shifted in the bed. Awareness swept through her, of what she'd done and with whom. She was still naked beneath the sheet. The sensation of the cloth against her bare skin reminded her of Hawk's touch during the night, of his hands bringing every inch of her skin to intense awareness. His fierce heat warmed her when they'd cooled down, keeping her close to him during the time they slept.

Flinging off the sheet, she rose and snatched her robe from the closet. Silly fantasies were fine for the midnight hours, but she had work to do.

* * *

As she dished up the eggs and pancakes for the men sitting around her breakfast table, she flicked a quick glance around. None of them appeared to be eyeing her any differently this morning. Walt still looked tired. Pepe swapped yarns with Matt and Jeremy. Only Hawk watched her. Like a hawk, she thought, almost giggling at the notion. He'd probably heard that line a million times before. Yet the more she thought about it, the more it described him. He was a hunter, seeking prey. She'd fallen into his claws and couldn't get loose. The only difference was she didn't want to get loose. At least not now.

"Well, best to get the day started," Walt said as he finished his coffee and set the cup down on the table. "Pepe, need you to check on those mares on the south end. Matt, you and Hawk can work on that water bore near—"

"No," Hawk interrupted calmly. He looked steadily at Walt.

The older man paused, looked puzzled. He flicked a glance at Amanda. Her gaze was on Hawk.

Trepidation began to build. What was he doing? She'd made Walt foreman, was Hawk now challenging that? Just because of last night? She swallowed and looked at Walt. He waited for her to make a decision. She hesitated as she met the gaze of every one of the men around the table. Hawk put her in an impossible position.

Clearing her throat, she turned to Walt. "I made Walt foreman, he's in charge." She couldn't look at Hawk. She didn't want to be in the middle of some power play. If he thought because she slept with him last night he could do whatever he wanted, she had to show him he could not. Heart beating rapidly, she nodded at Walt. She had made him foreman, she had to support him. She would not have his authority challenged before everyone.

"There's a storm coming in tonight. That hole in the barn needs repairing before it hits. You've already got a dozen bales of rotten hay because of leaks. You can't afford any more rain damage. I'll fix the roof this morning," Hawk said. Anger began to simmer around the edges. Dammit, she was the most pigheaded woman he knew. She'd slapped him in the face a week ago by making Walt foreman. She knew it then, and she knew it now. She could have asked why he refused before backing Walt.

Walt hesitated, then nodded. "Sounds fine. Pepe, you go with Matt to the bore and make sure it's cleaned out. Jeremy, you're with me this morning." Walt pushed back from the table and walked out of the room.

In only a moment, everyone followed him but Hawk. He sat at the table, his eyes never leaving Amanda.

"You had no right to embarrass Walt like that," she said when the screen door closed behind the last cowhand.

"We wouldn't be in this position if you hadn't made him foreman last week. We both know you did it just to get back at me. Walt's a good cowboy. He knows his job and does it well. But he's getting old, sugar. His arthritis bothers him in the mornings. And he didn't need to have a ton of responsibility dumped on him while you got back at me."

"I did not—"

"Be honest, Amanda. You had the right of it. I was way out of line and you jerked me back. But, sugar, don't punish the wrong man. Walt's not up to being foreman. I suspect you've told him what everyone is to do—he's still carrying out your orders."

"I own the place," she replied coldly.

"Sure you do. But neither one of you gave a thought to the repairs that are needed. You're still treading water, trying to keep from drowning. You need a foreman who can direct this place with a firm idea of what the priorities are."

"Like you, I suppose. Just because you slept with me last night doesn't give you the right to take over." She stood and snatched at the dirty dishes, dumping them in the sink.

Hawk rose and followed her, his own hands full. He placed the plates and silverware carefully in the water splashing into the sink.

"Let's get one thing straight. I didn't just sleep with you last night. I'm not into one-night stands. I would say more we are sleeping together now."

She stared at the soapy bubbles rising. *Sleeping together.* He hadn't wanted just a one-night stand. She felt so thankful her legs grew weak.

"Amanda?"

She turned, surprised to find him so close to her. His heat enveloped her and she could smell his unique scent. Hunger flared; she longed to taste him again, to feel those strong arms around her.

"I'm not out to undermine anyone. I'm looking out for your best interests. Your barn roof needs repair and today's the last time to do it before the storm hits."

She nodded. "I should have thought of it."

Brushing his lips against hers, he smiled down into

her serious face. "As long as someone did, no harm done."

"Mommy, is breakfast ready?" Joey trailed into the kitchen, still looking sleepy in his pajamas.

Amanda turned from the sink, from Hawk, and smiled at her son. "Sure is, honey. Have a seat. The others have eaten, so it's just you. Did you sleep well? You sure slept in late."

Hawk greeted the boy and left. Amanda felt tired when he was gone. And dispirited. She shouldn't have forced Walt to become foreman, especially just to get back at Hawk. She had put an unfair burden on the older man. Yet what was she to do now? She wouldn't insult him by taking the job away. She'd have to make it work.

Maybe he was finally learning some control, Hawk thought an hour later as he pulled up broken shingles. Amanda made him madder than anyone he'd been around lately, yet he was able to hold on to the anger, contain it. Work things out without becoming physical. Not that he would ever hit a woman. But sometimes he wanted to put his fist through the wall around her.

He couldn't fault her for distancing herself from him this past week. He'd hurt her. He knew enough about women to understand that. And maybe he could have handled the situation a bit better this morning. But he'd wanted to push her. Last night had meant a lot to him. He wanted her even as he yanked up the damaged shingles and tossed them to the ground. He had wanted her at breakfast. Had wanted to kiss her until they both went up in smoke, and damn the opinion of the others.

But more than anything, he wanted her to trust him again. To demonstrate that by siding with him. She had backed Walt this morning. If the older man had insisted he work on the bore, she would have sided with Walt. Which was right from a business point of view, but dammit he didn't feel in the least business-like around Amanda Williams.

He worked on the damaged roof until he reached solid trusses. He repaired the supports, tossing the rotting ones down on the ground. Climbing down the ladder, he went to the back of the barn where Walt had mentioned there were some more shingles. Rummaging through them, he found a few. But they were old, cracked and not worth anything but kindling.

He glanced up. The hole had to be three feet across, directly above the hayloft. He had to close it off before the rain came—even if it meant a trip into town to get more shingles.

"Hi, Hawk. Can I help?" Joey walked into the barn and looked up at the hole in the roof.

"Hi, partner. I think I better do the roofing work myself. You can hold the ladder for me when I go up again, though."

"Okay." Joey smiled and kicked one of the broken shingles. "Whatcha doing now? When are you going back up the ladder?"

"Not for a little while. I need to go into town and get some more shingles. These won't work. When I get back you can hold the ladder. How's that?" Hawk ruffled the boy's hair, remembering how Amanda's had felt last night.

"Can I go with you?"

"I'm just riding into town to get the shingles and

then coming right back. I'm not going anywhere exciting,'' Hawk said, heading out toward the truck.

"I can ride with you. I never get to go to town."

"You go ask your mother," Hawk said. He remembered Amanda's adamant restriction about Joey's going to Tagget. And how he had asked her to reconsider. He thought she made too much of the situation, but the boy was hers. And he'd follow her decision.

"Okay. Wait right here. I'll go ask her. Wait right here," Joey said, running toward the house, looking back over his shoulder as if Hawk would disappear.

Hawk smiled and leaned against the truck, soaking up the warmth of the morning sun. He knew the rain would cool things down a bit, but the sun felt good against his skin, through his shirt. He wished he could go get Amanda and take her riding. Maybe they could go down near the river, have a picnic. Make love in the shade of some tree.

Whoa, he snapped his eyes open, feeling the stirring of arousal. Time enough to see her later. He had a roof to patch.

"She said yes!" Joey jumped off the steps and ran toward the truck as fast as his little legs could carry him. "She said yes I can ride with you!" He beamed up at Hawk.

Startled, Hawk looked toward the house. She'd said yes? She'd trusted him with her precious son? Trusted him to take him into town. Damn, but that beat her siding with him in the confrontation he tried to provoke this morning. She trusted him with Joey!

"Well, partner, let's ride. Sooner we're gone, sooner we'll be back."

* * *

Hawk turned into the ranch driveway with a deep feeling of satisfaction. He glanced at Joey, still sticky from the ice-cream cone they'd bought. He should clean him up a bit before his mother saw him. Smiling at the happy expression on the boy's face, he turned back to the drive.

In the truck bed were the two stacks of shingles, charged to the ranch. Smugly pleased he was able to make the man see the light, he couldn't wait to tell Amanda she now had credit at one store in town. Though he wouldn't tell her quite how he'd gotten them to reluctantly agree. She would undoubtedly think he'd forced the man just because he'd threatened to wipe the floor with him.

He didn't have long to wait to tell her. She was waiting on the steps when the truck came to a halt. Her eyes flashing, she marched across the yard, glancing from Joey to Hawk.

"Where have you been?" she asked as Hawk cut the engine.

He climbed out, slammed the door behind him. "Town. Needed more shingles."

Her face paled. "You took Joey to town. I told you I didn't want him going to town."

"I sent him in to ask you if he could go. He said you said he could."

She looked at her son, grinning from the truck. "He asked me if he could ride with you. I thought he meant on the horse, like he's done before." Glaring at him, she put her fists on her hips. "Hawk, you knew I didn't want him in town. Dammit, I told you loud and clear."

"And if I remember correctly, I told you to think

over that decision and let the boy go in once in a while. I thought when he came back and said yes that you had done just that. That you had trusted me with your son."

"It's not a question of trust, it's the entire problem with Tagget and its small-minded citizens."

"Nothing happened. We got the shingles, stopped for a quick ice-cream cone and came home."

"That's all?"

"Mommy, we went to town." Joey leaned out the driver's door. Hawk reached around and pulled him through the window and set him on the ground.

"I can see you did," she replied, eyeing the dried chocolate ice cream around his mouth. "And had an ice cream, I see."

He nodded. "And some old lady wanted to take me, but Hawk wouldn't let her. And then the man took her away and she was crying."

"Hell!" He hoped the boy wouldn't bring that up before he could talk to Amanda.

Nine

"What woman?" Amanda asked.

Hawk glanced at the boy, gazing up between them. "Not in front of Joey."

Amanda nodded. "Joey, go inside and wash your face. You've got chocolate all over it."

"Okay." He scampered off toward the house. When he went inside, Amanda turned back to Hawk.

"What woman?"

"I think she was Mrs. Pembroke." He reached out to touch her and she stepped back.

"Where did this happen?"

"On the sidewalk outside the ice-cream store. We were coming out, and she saw us. She stared at Joey like she'd seen a ghost. Then she tried to talk to the boy, but I picked him up and we left."

"Joey looks exactly like Bobby Jack," she said slowly, her eyes glazing as she stared beyond Hawk.

"Nobody said anything that could hurt the boy. No one commented on him within our hearing. And he had a good time. He helped me pick out the shingles, and then we discussed the possibility of building him a swing in the barn. That way he could use it in the rain."

Hawk stepped closer and encircled her neck with his hand. Shaking her gently, he looked into her worried eyes. "The boy had a good time, sugar. No harm done."

"I guess." She shrugged, more aware of the man before her than her earlier concerns about Joey's reception in town. "He did seem happy."

"You must not feed him enough ice cream, he loves it." Slowly he drew her closer until he could kiss her. His tongue skimmed across her lips and she opened to him without hesitation. Relief warred with desire as he drew her against him. He'd been afraid she'd say no. That she'd be angry he'd taken the boy to town, that he'd challenged her that morning. And maybe she was, but she didn't hold a grudge.

"Umm, I don't think he's the only one who likes ice cream. I can still taste the chocolate," she murmured against his mouth, her hands lifting to cup his face.

"If it wouldn't have melted, I would have brought you one."

"Maybe next time I'll go in with you." Her arms slid around his neck, and she initiated the next kiss.

A puff of wind swirled around them, kicking up dust and grit.

"I best get that roof fixed. The hole I left is a mite bigger than the leak was to start with."

"Can I help?"

"Now you sound like Joey. He's going to hold the ladder for me. What do you want to hold?"

Her eyes gleamed and the smile that lit her face touched him to his toes.

"Don't say it, sugar. You go up in the loft and push the rotten bales over. We'll take them out and scatter them in the corral."

"Okay. And I was just going to say I could hold your hammer for you."

"Right!" He swatted her on the bottom as she turned and her laughter rang out. It was good to hear.

It proved to be a race between Hawk and the approaching storm. He glanced at the darkening sky from time to time, but mostly concentrated on rebuilding the roof. He couldn't go any faster and the storm would arrive when it arrived. He worked steadily, hoping to finish before the rain. Resigned to finish the repair today no matter what.

He beat the storm with ten minutes to spare. He had already replaced the tools and ladder when the first sprinkles began. Climbing up into the loft, he stood beneath the repaired roof and searched for any leaks. In only moments the rain beat down heavily and he smiled in satisfaction. Nary a drop in sight.

Amanda had cleared the loft of the rotting hay, only the few remaining bales of clean hay remained. The place smelled so familiar. With the scent of rain mixed in with horse, cattle and hay, Hawk knew he was home. He never wanted to work as anything but a cowboy or rancher. Didn't want to be lured into an office job by some money-hungry woman.

And the Royal Flush Ranch looked better every day. With his capital he could make it a showplace, repaint the buildings, expand the herd. Hire some more men, take the work load off Amanda. Give her time to spend on her horses and to spend with Joey without feeling she was stretched to the limit.

He resettled his hat and descended the loft ladder. He needed to plan better how to approach her a second time. She had not been receptive with his first offer.

"You were right, it's pouring out." She greeted him when he reached the barn floor. Wearing a long pink slicker, she dripped water wherever she stepped.

"The roof's tight. No more hay spoiled by water."

"Thank you. I'm sorry about this morning."

"No problem. Come talk to me while I saddle Geronimo."

"Saddle him? Why? You can't be going out in this?"

"The others are out there, may need some help. Work doesn't stop because of a little rain," he said, hefting a saddle over his shoulder and snagging the reins.

"But you've done your task for the day."

"Sugar, there's more than one thing to do a day. I'll ride out and see if the others need help."

She took off her hat and shook it, unwilling to let him know she had hoped he would come back to the house with her, spend the afternoon together. She could heat some hot chocolate, they could sit and talk. And maybe share a kiss or two—nothing more with Joey underfoot.

She sighed.

Hawk eyed her as he tied the horse to the post so he could get him saddled.

"Something wrong?"

"No. I just thought we might spend a little time together."

"I plan to spend a lot more than a little time tonight. I'll stay when I come in for dinner," he said, brushing the horse, flicking a quick glance over his shoulder. He didn't want to take anything for granted—he was still unsure where he stood with Amanda.

"Okay," she said. "I'll head back inside, then. I don't want Joey getting into mischief."

"One for the road?" he asked.

She paused, uncertainty growing.

"A kiss, sugar, just a kiss."

"Somehow, cowboy, your kisses are anything but *just a kiss*." She sashayed over to him and tilted her chin until her lips were the right angle, daring him with her eyes.

Hawk leaned over, keeping his eyes open and on hers. He brushed her lips, came again. This time his tongue parted her lips slightly.

Amanda's breath caught. His dark blue gaze held hers captive. His kiss was more potent that it had a right to be. Especially light as it had been.

"That'll tide me over," he said gruffly, turning back to the horse. Dammit, it did nothing but inflame his libido. He wanted to pull her into an empty stall, fluff up the hay and drag her underneath him until they were both sated. A light little kiss like that no more satisfied him than a handshake would. He wanted much more.

"You're going to wear a slicker, aren't you?" she asked.

"Yes, boss lady. I'll get my slicker on the way out. Go in the house."

"Bossy," she muttered as she turned and headed for the house. She would make a wonderful dinner for them all. And a sinfully rich chocolate dessert. Then if Joey would cooperate and go to be early, she and Hawk would have the evening to themselves. Amanda smiled in joyful anticipation.

It was a tired group of cowboys who trooped into the kitchen that evening. The rain had settled into a steady drizzle that didn't look to let up before morning. They had all changed before coming to eat.

Amanda dished up the hearty soup to start, glad she'd been able to stay inside with Joey. Hiring Matt and Jeremy had been a risk, but well worth it today.

They had just begun to eat when the phone rang. Amanda rose to answer it.

"Matt, it's for you."

The young cowboy looked up. "Is it all right if I take the call?"

"Sure, you can use the office phone if you like," she said.

"Thanks." He hurried down the hall. When Amanda heard his voice on the line, she quietly hung up.

They had moved on to the main course of roast beef and rice when Matt returned. He sat down to finish his soup.

"I appreciate your letting me take the call. I didn't know if I could use the phone or not. I should have found out earlier."

"Sure, anytime," Amanda replied.

"Who's calling you at dinner?" Walt asked, curious.

"Karen Parker," Matt replied, suddenly very interested in his soup.

"He's sweet on her," Jeremy said, smirking.

"That's right," Matt said, looking up. His gaze narrowed on his friend. "Want to make something of it?"

"Not me." Jeremy shook his head, then looked at Amanda. "That's the main reason we came here looking for work. Matt didn't want to leave the Tagget area. If you weren't hiring, we'd have had to look farther afield and he's sweet on Karen."

"She knows you, Amanda," Matt said, changing the subject. "She said the two of you went to school together."

"That's right," Amanda said shortly. She remembered Karen.

He hesitated, then plunged on. "Karen says she hasn't seen you in years. Almost forgot you lived here."

Amanda nodded. "It has been years, I guess."

"Ain't surprising. Amanda never leaves the place," Walt grumbled.

"I was just in town a few weeks ago. That's where I ran into Hawk, remember?" she said.

"One odd time, boss. Before that, how long since you went to Tagget? Right after Jonas died," Pepe said.

Matt looked at the older cowboy, then at Amanda, puzzlement evident.

Hawk watched the younger man, satisfied the way the conversation was going. Matt was too smart to let things slide with this kind of information. Before long he'd come to some interesting conclusions. And just maybe help Hawk in his quest to change the town's opinion of Amanda.

"Karen said she never saw you at any of the places people normally go, like the café, the movies, the ice-cream shop."

Amanda shook her head. "Anyone want more meat?"

"Not surprising. Those are places young people go on dates. Amanda doesn't date," Walt said.

Matt and Jeremy looked at him.

"Never has since she moved here, anyway," Pepe added brusquely.

Hawk started to enjoy himself. He leaned back in his chair, studying the others at the table. Amanda was growing flustered. He knew she didn't like to talk about herself.

Walt and Pepe ate steadily through their meal. They didn't realize exactly what was happening. Finally Matt put down his spoon and looked at the table for a moment. Then he took a deep breath.

"Amanda, I think you should know there's talk in town about you. It's not very nice. In fact, before I started work here I heard some of it and that's why I made that crack out by the fence." He looked up at her, color staining his cheeks. "But I mentioned it to Karen right after you gave me the job and she said it was nothing but nasty spite talking. There were a lot of people in town that didn't give it any credence. And one reason was because no one ever saw you around."

"Because she doesn't go into town," Walt repeated patiently.

"And because she doesn't date," Matt repeated.

"But some of the talk has suggested that she…she does date," he finished, glancing at Joey.

"Sometimes people lie," Hawk said abruptly.

"Or exaggerate things out of proportion," Amanda said slowly.

Hawk met her gaze. "They out-and-out lied, sugar. Don't try to excuse it."

Matt spoke again. "Karen said to tell you if you come to town, to stop by the hardware store and say hi. She, um, let her boss know what she thought about the entire situation after Hawk opened the door this morning."

Amanda's eyes widened at that. "What happened this morning?"

Matt looked at Hawk.

"You could have kept your mouth shut about the last part," Hawk said sharply.

"What happened this morning?" she repeated.

"I'll tell you later." Hawk looked at Joey, watching with fascination as the adults talked. "When little pitchers aren't around."

"What happened this morning?" she demanded as soon as Joey had been put to bed and she rejoined Hawk in the living room. He had lit a fire in the fireplace. It was too warm to need one, so he'd opened the window slightly, enough to let in the cool night air, yet keep the rain out.

Hawk reached out and caught her hand, pulling her down into his lap. "Joey asleep?"

"He will be in another minute or so. He was almost there when I left the room. What—"

He laid his finger across her lips. "I talked the man at the hardware store into granting credit for purchasing the shingles, that's all. Mentioned a bit about discrimination and lawsuits, nothing much.''

Her eyes widened. ''That's not all, is it?''

''It's all I'm going to talk about tonight. I didn't stay to talk.'' With that, he covered his mouth with hers, leaning over until she lay on the sofa and he half covered her.

Amanda wanted to know more but knew the minute his lips touched hers that she would hear no more that night. And she didn't care. She encircled his neck, pulling him against her as she opened her mouth and kissed him back.

He kissed her and petted her and drove her to distraction. When she fumbled for his belt, his hands closed over hers and drew them away. Resting his cheek against hers, he rumbled in her ear, ''There's time for that when we go to bed. I just want to play with you for a while. Isn't it fun?''

''You're driving me crazy with wanting,'' she said, turning her head to kiss his jaw, her lips rubbing over the slight roughness of his beard stubble.

''So it will be the hotter when we get to bed. I'm not immune to you, either, you know.''

She did know. She felt the evidence against her belly.

''So when do we go to bed?'' she asked, trailing her fingertips over his back, beneath his shirt. The heat from his skin almost burned her. She liked the lean sculptured feel of him, wanted to rub her hands all over him. Learn every single inch.

''Impatient little thing, aren't you?'' He nibbled her jaw, kissed the tender spot behind her ear, tugged on her lobe.

''Hawk, I don't think I can wait for bed.'' She

moved against him, tension creating a terrific need that she wanted assuaged. He might think it was fun, but she was burning up with a need for him that wouldn't be satisfied by kisses. She wanted more.

He raised his head and grinned at her. "So much for my technique of drawing things out."

She touched his jaw, her eyes gazing up into his. "Draw them out in bed, cowboy. I want you very much."

"Oh, sugar." He kissed her hard, then rose and scooped her up. In less than three minutes they were in her room. He wasn't even breathing hard, she noticed, her own breath shallow and erratic.

When he slowly lowered her to the floor, he made sure her body rubbed his all the way down. She looped her arms around him, pressing herself against his chest, her lips already along his jaw, tasting his skin, feeling the slight abrasion of his day-long beard.

"Thought you wanted the bed," he murmured, his teeth nipping her earlobe.

"I do, but can we get there without letting go?" she asked.

She felt his chuckle and tightened her hold. Her lips found his and Amanda was seared by his kiss. It went on and on and the world spun around. Or maybe it was them. Suddenly she was falling. Hawk's heavy weight pressed her into the softness of her mattress. His legs tangled with hers, his arms held her hard against him.

Amanda couldn't think, she could only feel the starburst of sensations that exploded inside her. She wanted to protest when his mouth left hers, but the touch of his lips on her neck had her arching, offering herself to him.

Dimly she felt the buttons on her shirt come loose. Hawk slipped the cotton from her shoulders, pulling it off her arms. She didn't feel the coolness of the night, only the heat that poured through her at his touch.

"Amanda."

Opening her eyes, she gazed up at him. "What?"

"Just Amanda. I like your name."

Smiling, she reached out to unfasten the buttons on his shirt. "I like Hawk. It's a perfect name. You have a killer smile."

"Lift up and let's get these jeans off."

It took the two of them a long time to discard the jeans. Kisses and touches and hugs interrupted. Finally they lay beside each other in the narrow bed with nothing between them. Amanda thought she might feel awkward, but she felt anything but. With the murmured words Hawk whispered, she felt beautiful, desirable, utterly feminine.

His hands skimmed across her heated skin, from breast to belly to thigh. She moved against him, reveling in his touch, in the sensations that shimmered through her at every stroke. Her own fingertips learned the differences in his body. He was hard, muscular, yet his skin was smooth and even. Except where the wiry hair covered his chest, then dove downward.

Tentatively she touched a flat male nipple, shivering in surprised delight at his gasp.

"Do it again," he growled.

She complied, almost mindless with the sensations he brought her. Was she doing the same thing to him? Daringly she leaned down and lapped it with her tongue.

"Lady, you're driving me wild."

"Good, you drove me wild hours ago." Days ago, an eternity ago.

Hawk slowed his hand, drawing lazy patterns against her skin, his lips following his hands, capturing one rosy tip and sucking gently. When Amanda thought she would scream in frustration and desire, he gently pushed her legs apart and covered her. Slowly, slowly he moved against her, pushing into the warmth that waited.

She held still, savoring the feel of his body on hers, in hers. She knew there would be more, just seconds away, but for the moment she wanted to savor—

Hawk began to move and Amanda wrapped her arms and legs around him and met his every thrust. Soon they moved as one, climbing higher and higher until the earth seemed to burst into flames and sparkles and pure light. They rode the peak together until they crashed down on the far side.

When Amanda awoke, she lay half under Hawk. He was still asleep, his breathing deep and even. His hot body warmed her more than any blanket ever could. He had opened the window when they'd finished making love, to cool them down, he'd said. The fresh clean smell of rain filled the room, the air cool and a bit damp. She didn't mind. She loved being with him.

Turning just a little, she kissed his bare chest.

"Don't waste them there, sugar," he mumbled, gathering her even closer and nuzzling her neck.

"I thought you were asleep."

"I was. You were, too."

"Ummm."

"Are you cold? Do you want me to draw up the covers?" he asked, rubbing one big hand along her side, down to her hip, to her thigh. Her skin felt cool to the touch.

"I could never be cold with you half over me. You're like a furnace."

"If you were cold, I know a way to warm you up." His mouth trailed kisses along her jaw, finding her lips.

"Talk to me a bit, instead," she said a few minutes later.

"About what?"

"Where you're from, what you did before coming here." Not where you're going, she thought with a pang. She didn't want to think about that. She wanted to know more about him, not anticipate a future when he would be gone.

"Not much to tell. I grew up in Cripple Creek, Colorado. My dad had a ranch down there. He sold it when I was in high school, moved to Denver. I worked ranches, did some rodeoing. Came here."

"Wow, your life in twenty-five words or less," she remarked.

He chuckled. "Not much to tell, is it?"

"Were you ever married?"

He stilled. "No." His voice grew harder.

"Why not? You're in your early thirties, good-looking for a cowboy, and work hard. You could support a wife."

He pulled back and stared at her, trying to see her features in the dark. "I just turned thirty a couple of weeks ago," he said, insulted she'd thought him older.

Amanda snuggled closer, biting her lower lip to

keep from laughing aloud. "Sorry, my mistake. You seem so mature and…and experienced, I just assumed you were older."

"Is that like saying I'm stodgy?"

"No! And I said early thirties—thirty is very early."

"Maybe to a baby like you at twenty-three thirty does seems old, but it's not."

"Is this your way of avoiding my question about why you never married?" she asked.

He sighed. "No. I just don't see myself married. Haven't met a woman I'd want to be tied to for life. And I've seen what a woman can do to a man."

"What do you mean?" Intrigued by the bitterness in his tone, she wanted to know more. Had he been hurt once by a woman?

"My mother left my dad when I was a kid. Took him for everything he had. Then a few years later he married again. Think a man would learn, wouldn't you? Ellen harped on him constantly that the ranch wasn't good enough, that he could make more money in a city. So he sold the place, moved and still couldn't satisfy her. When she left, she took a hefty settlement with her."

"All women aren't like that. Sounds like your dad had a run of bad luck," she said softly.

"Hmm. Maybe, but I don't plan to throw my hand in to find out."

She knew he was not staying. He'd been up front and clear about that from the beginning. Yet until he told her about his father, she had hoped maybe, just maybe, he'd stay. Hoped one day she could tell him how much she loved him.

Love? Yes, she loved him! That's why she couldn't

bear the thought of his leaving. Why even when he'd said the words to wound her, she'd let him stay. Wanted him to stay. It wasn't just for the sake of the ranch. It was for her sake as well.

Her heart pounded and sadness filled her. She would miss him so much when he left. She had waited a lifetime for love, and it was not to be with Hawk.

"I'm a little cool. I would like the blanket," she murmured, turning a little away from him. The chill came from within, not from the cool fresh air. But she could never tell him that.

She was uncertain what to do. She had not shared herself with him with any promise from Hawk that it would lead anywhere. She had wanted him, he had wanted her and they had made love. Numerous times, now. The fact she loved him had no bearing on the situation. She would keep silent, enjoy his company for as long as he gave it to her and not cause a scene when he left.

"Amanda?"

"What?"

"I could warm you up better than a blanket," he said softly, his hand featherlight against her ribs.

She smiled and turned to him, hugging him tightly. "I'd like that a lot."

Two days later Amanda was working at her desk when Walt knocked on the doorframe. "Got a minute, Amanda?"

"Sure, Walt, come in. What's up?"

He sat down, dropped his hat on his knee and stared at her. "I tried my best, honey, but I'm just not cut out to be a foreman. I don't want to do it anymore."

She sighed. "I know, Walt. Thank you for taking it on. I'm sorry I pushed so hard. I thought it might work."

"No, honey, you thought to put that young Hawk Blackstone in his place. You know that, I know that and Hawk knows it. If you want a bang-up foreman, one who will know what to do all the time, and how to get the most from the men, give the job to Hawk."

"He's not staying long enough."

"How long's long enough? He seems pretty content here to me."

"Until his real estate agent calls and tells him he's found him a ranch."

"Might not happen this year or the next, either. Use his talents while you can, Amanda."

She nodded. "I'll talk to him," she promised.

Hawk and Pepe were working on the corral railings that afternoon when Joey came running from the house. "Hawk, Hawk, come quick. Mommy's mad. She's yelling and crying. Hurry." The little boy paused by the fence, gasping for breath, his face fearful.

"What's the matter?" Hawk asked, vaulting over the railing and hunkering down beside the boy. "Take a deep breath, now tell me."

"It's Mommy, she's yelling and crying and everything! You have to come now!"

Hawk rose and strode swiftly toward the house. As he drew near, he could hear Amanda screaming inside. He ran.

She paced the office, a crumpled paper in her hand,

tears streaming down her cheeks, swearing up a storm.

"You heartless bastard," she yelled when she spied Hawk in the doorway. "You low-life son-of-a-*bitch*." She launched herself across the room and raised her fist to strike him. "It's all your fault!" she screamed.

"Hey!" He caught her fist and turned her around. Pulling her back tight against his chest, he danced out of the way of her heel when she tried to kick him. "Easy, Amanda. Stop that!"

"Let me go you arrogant, self-centered snake in the grass."

"Stop it!" he roared, tightening his grip around her waist. "Stop it now!"

She sagged in his arms and began to sob. Turning her around, Hawk pulled her against his chest, holding her as she wept.

"Is Mommy all right?" Joey asked fearfully from the door.

"She will be. Why don't you go in the kitchen and get her a glass of water. Don't rush so you spill it. We'll wait right here for you," Hawk said.

When Joey disappeared, Hawk held her with one arm, rubbing her back with his hand. "What's the matter with you, Amanda? You scared the bejesus out of your son, and didn't do a bad job with me, either."

"It's all your fault, Hawk, and I'll never forgive you. Never, never, never," she wailed.

"Hush now, you're going to make yourself sick. Can you stop crying?"

"My life's ending and you want me to calm down?" she cried.

Fear clutched Hawk. What did she mean?

He tilted back her head, brushing away her tears as more followed.

"Don't touch me!" she ordered, stepping back. "You've ruined everything, you arrogant know-it-all. I should never have offered you a job. I should have insisted you leave when you insulted me. But no, I have to let you stay just because—"

"Mommy, I brought you some water. Do you want it?" Joey stood in the doorway, his eyes wide with worry.

Amanda looked at her son. Dashing away the tears with her fists, she nodded and sank to her knees as he carefully brought the glass to her.

"Thank you, sweetheart." She took a sip and tried to smile, but the tears kept falling. She ran a shaky hand over his head. "I'm sorry if I scared you, Joey. I didn't mean to." She gathered him up and hugged him, resting her head on his hair.

"What's going on, Amanda?" Hawk asked coldly.

She glared at him. "None of your damned business. Get out. Get off my ranch and don't ever come back."

"Like hell I will. For God's sake, Amanda, you're almost hysterical. If something's wrong, tell me. Maybe I can fix it."

"You fixed it just fine. I told you not to take him to town. I told you!" She rocked back on her heels, trying to smile at Joey. "I'm going to be okay, honey. Sorry I got so upset. Want to go get me some tissues?"

Joey nodded and scampered off, anxious to help.

Hawk drew a deep breath and reached out for the paper clutched in her fist. Slowly, so as not to tear it, he loosened her fingers and drew the paper out.

Glancing at it, he bit back an oath. Anger rose at the injustice of it all.

"Joey, your mother's going to be fine. Why don't you go help Pepe with the rest of the fence. Tell him I won't be out for a few minutes," Hawk said when the little boy returned with a fistful of tissue. He was hard put to clamp down on his initial impulse—to go to town and beat the tar out of Robert Pembroke.

"Are you okay, Mommy?" Joey asked, patting her shoulder.

Amanda tried to smile and nod. It was a pathetic attempt but successful enough to satisfy her son. "I'll be fine. You go and help Pepe."

Hawk reached out and gripped her arm, drawing her to her feet. She shrugged off his hand.

"You can rail at me all you want, but not now. We have to stop this idiocy before it goes any further," he said.

"*We* don't have to do anything. I told you to leave." Her fists on her hips, she glared at him. Her eyes were red-rimmed, her cheeks still flushed.

"Sugar, there's no way in hell I'd leave you in this mess. Now sit down over there and we'll discuss this."

"What's to discuss? Robert Pembroke is petitioning the courts for full custody of his grandson. The same grandson they ignored and denied for five years. Now that they've seen him, seen that he's the spitting image of Bobby Jack, suddenly they're willing to acknowledge that their son did father him. And they want him."

"You're his mother. The courts aren't just going to take him away from his mother to give him to people who are strangers to him,'' Hawk said reasonably.

"Read the rest of the complaint. I'm supposed to be unfit. My reputation is well-known. I'm living in sin with some cowboy.'' Tears spilled over again.

Hawk skimmed the paper again. "It doesn't say all that.''

"That will be their case, I know it. But the part of a stable family environment, with no financial worries, that part is very clear.''

"Then we'll fix it so they don't have a case. You aren't going to lose your son, Amanda. I promise.''

"Just go away, Hawk. I don't need any more help from you.''

"You do, and you're going to get it. You are not going to lose your son!''

"Easy for you to say.''

He leaned over her, his face so close to hers she could see nothing but the dark anger in his eyes. "I always keep my promises, Amanda. You can count on that.''

Within the hour Hawk and Amanda were in the truck on the way to Thermopolis. Hawk had called his brother, who had recommended an attorney specializing in family law. She agreed to see them that day as a favor to Alec Blackstone.

Hawk drove swiftly, competently. He was concerned about Amanda. She looked like death warmed over, pale and listless once the first wave of anger passed. She hadn't said much since Alec had recommended the attorney. But the worry that settled over her disturbed him deeply. Hawk didn't like seeing it, and didn't like knowing she was partially correct. *He had caused it.*

If he had double-checked to make sure she had changed her mind about allowing her son into town, he would have known that was the last thing she wanted. And if they hadn't stopped for the ice-cream cone, they would not have run into the Pembrokes.

Amanda loved her son more than anything. And he had caused this distress. He felt like hell.

And he meant what he said—he would make sure the Pembrokes did not gain custody of her child. He wasn't sure how to keep that promise, but he would. One way or another.

Mitzy Howard, attorney-at-law, did not keep them waiting when they arrived at her office. She had them ushered straight in. With a sympathetic smile at Amanda, she shook her hand warmly. "Now, don't worry. I know this is a shock, but we'll fight them every step of the way. After I talked with Alec, I contacted the opposing attorney and he faxed me all the material concerning the case. Let's discuss it, shall we?"

"Hawk Blackstone, ma'am." Hawk extended his hand, liking her firm grip.

"You look like your brother. Have a seat."

Amanda felt numb. She nodded and sat where indicated, her heart pounding in fear. Should she have left Joey at the ranch with Walt and Pepe? What if the Pembrokes showed up today and took him?

Ten

Mitzy Howard reviewed the various aspects of the case the Pembrokes had filed. Amanda answered all her questions, but couldn't help feeling that she was just going through the motions. The charges seemed overwhelming. She was almost sick with fear.

"We have a bit of work to do, but I think we can successfully defend this," Mitzy said, glancing at her notes.

"What's the worst aspect?" Hawk asked. "The fact that Joey doesn't go to school?"

"No, if Amanda's done the homeschooling right, as I'm sure she has, he will be on grade level when they test him. That's fine. Homeschooling is growing more and more popular. And the children usually do as well or even better than children in the public schools."

"Is it my reputation?" Amanda asked dully.

When Mitzy hesitated, Hawk spoke, "That's easily remedied. I suggest you subpoena every man in Tagget and asking him under oath if he's ever dated or slept with her. You won't find one. The only one who did was Bobby Jack Pembroke, when they were teenagers. And as she was underage at the time, I would think we could come up with a countersuit of statutory rape."

Mitzy grinned. "Wow, you don't pull any punches, do you? What an intriguing thought. Totally impractical, but intriguing." She shook her head. "Probably not necessary. We'll see if we need to go to such lengths later. The financial aspect is a bit troublesome. You seem to be operating on a shoestring. And the Pembrokes are extremely wealthy. They would be able to provide so many things for their grandson."

Hawk fisted his hands and started to say something, but the attorney continued.

"And then there is the argument of a dual parent home. Not that that would lend all that much weight, either. Many single parent homes are better for children."

"If that's a sticking block, we can solve that easily enough," Hawk said.

"How?" Mitzy looked surprised.

"Amanda and I will marry each other," he stated.

Amanda turned to look at him in total disbelief. "What did you say?"

"You and I can get married. That would give Joey a dual parent home. There's the matter of financial stability, as well. I told you I had some money in the bank. Enough to satisfy even the strictest judge."

"No," Amanda said.

"And it would solve any problem with the morals

issue. A lot of engaged couples anticipate their wedding night. We can be married by the end of the week," Hawk continued as if she had not spoken.

"No," she repeated, looking at Mitzy for assistance.

"Might not be a bad idea," the attorney said slowly.

"It's a horrible idea," Amanda said, seeing no help from that corner.

"Why?" Hawk asked, leaning back coolly in his chair, his right boot on his left knee. "Joey likes me and I like him. You and I get along, most of the time. And I want a part of your ranch."

Her head spun around. "That's the biggest part of all this, isn't it? You want part of the ranch. You tried looking for something, but this is easier, isn't it? How long before you try to kick me off it?"

"I've been looking for a spread, we all know that. Yours is not quite what I wanted, but I could make do. And I'm not looking to boot you off the place. It's yours, not mine." He watched her, curious to what she would say. Suddenly he wanted her to say yes. More than he'd ever wanted anything, he wanted her to say yes. "But maybe a bigger reason to get married is that you're right. If I hadn't taken Joey to town that day, the Pembrokes would not have seen his resemblance to their son. They would have continued to ignore him and you as they have for the past five years. And you would not have this problem."

"So we just have a marriage of convenience to give you part of my ranch and absolve you of your guilt? I don't think so."

"No one said anything about marriage of convenience. Unless you count it convenient to share a bed.

But I have to tell you, sugar, I want a bigger bed. That single of yours is too small for the rest of our lives.''

She flushed scarlet and avoided looking at the attorney. ''Shut up,'' she murmured to him.

He smiled, but his eyes were hard. ''Say yes, Amanda.'' He held her gaze, exerting as much energy as he could focus on her to say yes.

She felt trapped and scared. What if the Pembrokes were successful? What if they gained custody of her son? She couldn't bear that. She could stand anything else but that. Even marriage to a man who didn't love her.

If she dare let herself dream, she would have dreamed he stayed, they married and lived happily ever after. But she had lost her ability to dream a long time ago. She had to be practical and think of Joey. For Joey's sake, she would do anything..

''All right,'' she grumbled. The weight that lifted from her shoulders amazed her. She blinked and looked at him. He smiled like a cat with a canary. Tears threatened again. She wanted him to stay, but not like this, trapped into marriage because of guilt and greed.

He looked at the attorney. ''Will that clear it up?''

''I think it will certainly counter every argument they've filed, but we still have to go through the motions. The sooner you get married the better. The county will send in someone to test Joey, visually inspect the home, things like that. We'll stall the testing and home inspections as long as possible. Make sure everything shows to its best advantage. But it looks as if it will just be a case of going through the motions before we see the judge. You aren't going to lose your son, Amanda.''

''What if the judge is one of Robert Pembroke's cronies?'' Amanda asked, afraid to be reassured. Afraid to trust Hawk or Mitzy or anyone. She had depended on herself for so long, she didn't trust anyone.

''We'll request a change of venue. I'll request Judge Hartwell. She's a strong proponent of the child being in the best environment, not the most wealthy. Don't worry, we'll fight them and win.''

Amanda's cheeks were warm with color when she and Hawk headed toward home. In the back of the pickup truck, hanging over the sides, was a king-size bed, mattress, headboard, frame. She felt as if everyone in Thermopolis stared at her, knowing exactly what she and Hawk would be doing on that very bed before long.

''You don't have to marry me,'' she said as they reached the highway. There had to be other ways to fight this battle. Once she had some time to think, maybe she could come up with alternatives.

''It's settled,'' he said, reaching over and taking her hand. Lacing his fingers through hers, he rested their linked hands on his thigh. ''Do you think Joey will like having me for a dad?''

If she didn't already know Hawk was as self-confident as they came, she would think she heard hesitancy in his tone, uncertainty almost.

''Of course. He already follows you around like you're a god or something. But what about when you leave?''

''I'm not leaving.''

He was going to stay? Her heart lifted for a moment. Then crashed down. Why was he doing this? Was it just to get part ownership in her ranch? She couldn't believe that. It was not a showplace, some cash cow. It was a hard-up ranch barely making ends meet. It was going to take a lot of work for a number of years before it would be the place she wanted.

"I thought you didn't believe in marriage," she tried.

"I didn't," he said.

"Then why—"

"Amanda, do you not want to marry me?"

She swallowed and tried to think. Of course she wanted to marry him. She wanted to love him all his days. But she wanted him to love her in return, and he didn't. What kind of marriage would it be, lopsided and uneven? Would her love fade after years of being ignored, or would she love him all her life, even if he didn't love her in return?

Yet if they didn't marry, there would be nothing to hold him. He'd get a call from the real estate agent and be off for a place of his own. Married, she would have him always.

"Yes, I want to marry you," she said at last.

"It's settled then," he said. He had never planned to marry, until their ride into Thermopolis. His feeling guilty about being the cause of the suit first planted the idea. The attorney's support strengthened his idea. And he couldn't help feel Amanda would need more help as the years went on. The ranch and her son were too much responsibility for one person. This way, he'd have his ranch and make up for putting Joey in jeopardy.

He liked Joey. In fact, he was crazy about the kid.

He hoped he could be a better father to the boy than his father had been to him. He would make sure of it. But then, he didn't have to worry about his wife leaving him. It was her place to begin with, she would get nothing from him if they separated.

Not that they would split. His eyes were wide open and his mind set. He would marry Amanda, settle down and—

"Can we have kids?" he asked abruptly.

"What?"

"Children. I'd like to have a couple, if you would," he said.

Her heart melted and tears filled her eyes. *He wanted to have children with her.*

"Sure." She couldn't say anything more, her throat was too tight.

"I like Joey. If we had some others, he wouldn't be an only child."

"Oh, Hawk." She wanted to hug him, wanted to tell him how much she loved him. To share the joy in her heart at his diffident words. But she couldn't. He proposed marriage to assuage his guilt, to gain part of her property and…and maybe to have kids. She wouldn't burden him with emotions he didn't want. She already had more than she'd ever expected.

"Then we'll do it Friday."

"Friday? That's so soon." Amanda had scarcely adjusted to the idea that they would marry, now he wanted the wedding on Friday!

"Might as well get it over with as soon as possible."

Get it over with. Of course, for him it was mere expediency to thwart the custody suit. She swallowed hard. She had best get used to the idea.

"Friday's fine," she said, tonelessly.

"I'll call this afternoon when we get back to make arrangements," Hawk said. "I want Alec to come. Shall we invite Mitzy too, to make sure she's kept up to speed?"

"Sure."

Hawk looked over at her. "Any friends you want there, besides the men on the ranch? Do you have a preacher, or shall I ask around?"

"Wait a minute, you're going too fast. Hawk, I thought we'd just zip into Thermopolis and find a judge and get married."

"Oh, no, sugar. We'll do it right and tight and before the entire town if needed. There won't be any question about our marriage that the Pembrokes can latch on to. We'll be married in Tagget and make sure everyone knows it!"

"No!"

He turned to her, one eye on the road. "Yes. Tagget is the closest town. We're going to start shopping there, giving our business to our neighbors. Time things got back to normal, sugar. Everything will work out, I promise."

"And your promises always come true?" she asked skeptically.

"Always. Now, do you have a preacher, or not?"

"I haven't been to church in years, except to bury Jonas. I guess Reverend Patterson would do it." Amanda's head was spinning. What was she doing?

When they reached the ranch, Hawk called Pepe and Jeremy to help him unload the bed. Knowing their curiosity about the big bed, it took Hawk only a minute to clear things up. Wide smiles accompanied their congratulations. Amanda felt almost as giddy as a bride and quickly escaped into the house to lead the way to the master bedroom.

They dismantled Jonas's old bed and stored it in the bunkhouse. Before long, they had set up the king-size bed in the master bedroom.

When the others left, Hawk surveyed the bedroom. It needed fixing up. But it would suffice until they got around to it. It was a big, airy room. The bed did not take up too much space; there was plenty of room for the dresser and the chairs along the windows.

"Needs cleaning." Amanda stood in the doorway and looked in.

"Yeah. And a new paint job and new curtains and rugs. But a quick cleaning will do until we get to everything." He walked over to her and brushed her lips with his.

"We'll move in on Friday," he said, already imagining her on the big mattress, her hair spread around her face, her arms reaching for him.

"Not tonight?"

"We're not married yet. I want this to be our wedding bed."

She nodded, touched by the unexpected romantic notion. Her rowdy, fighting cowboy had hidden depths.

"So Friday's the day?" she murmured, her heart racing. She was going to marry this man. Share her life with him. See him every morning and every evening. Share his bed until they died. Or was it temporary until the custody suit was settled and Hawk found his ranch? He didn't want to be married, he'd said so. How long would he stay?

"Come on, there's one other thing." He took her

hand and led her downstairs and into the office. Going to the desk he found a piece of paper and ripped off a strip. Taking her hand, he marked her ring size on the paper. "I'm getting the ring tomorrow."

She looked up at him shyly. "Would you wear one?" she asked.

"Sure would." He grinned down at her, slowly, his eyes dancing in amusement. "Want to make sure everyone knows I'm taken, eh?"

She shrugged, not wanting to admit to that very reason. Her heart swelled with excitement. "Then I'll go in with you." She cleared her throat and gazed out the window. "I, uh, don't have a dress, so if you're dead set on having this be more like a wedding, I'll have to get something."

"You don't have a dress? You must be the only woman I know who doesn't have a dress."

"Well, I left home with very little, and since I rarely go anywhere, I didn't see any need for dresses."

He cupped her chin in his palm and turned her to face him. "I'll buy you a hundred," he said huskily.

She smiled. "Silly, what would I do with a hundred dresses? I'd much rather have another mare."

"Done. What else?"

She gazed into his eyes. He was serious. "I don't mean that," she said slowly, bringing her hand up to grip his wrist. She could feel the steady pulse from his heart, and hers leaped in response. Would his very presence always engender this awareness, this intensity of feeling?

"I told you once before I wanted to buy into the Royal Flush. I didn't plan to acquire it by marriage.

I've money enough to do whatever you want done, sugar. You say the word.''

She didn't know what to say. There was so much that needed to be done, she didn't even know where to start. And how much money was enough? Could she ask for a new windmill in the valley toward the hills? Or a new mare whose lines would assure good foals? Or should she ask for new curtains in their bedroom?

''Well?''

''I'm thinking. How much money do you have?''

''You tell me what you want and I'll tell you when to stop,'' he teased.

She flushed. ''Nothing right now. Maybe when we're married.''

''That's not long now.'' He kissed her.

Amanda savored his touch, tasting him, feeling the strong beat of his heart beneath her fingertips. She knew she could count on this man for her whole life. Even if he never grew to love her, he would care for her and their children. He was good with Joey, good with Walt and Pepe. He would never let her down.

''Oh, mushy stuff,'' Joey said from the door.

They broke apart and turned to the boy.

''Yeah, mushy stuff. Were you good while we were gone?'' Hawk asked, looking at the boy differently now. In two days Joey would be his son. He was just a bit scared.

''I helped Pepe. But I could have gone with you and gotten an ice cream.''

Hawk raised an eyebrow and looked smugly at Amanda. The kid was crazy for ice cream.

She grinned. ''We'll get you one on Friday.'' Taking a deep breath, she knelt down and opened her arms for Joey. He walked over and hugged her.

"On Friday Hawk and I are going to get married. Then he'll be your daddy. Will you like that?" she said, studying his face to gauge his reaction.

Joey turned and looked up, way up, to Hawk. He smiled and nodded. "Do I get to call you Daddy?"

"You bet, partner." Hawk reached down and picked up the little boy, hugging him gently, then settling him on his hip. "I don't have much experience with kids, son, but I'll do my best to be a good dad, Joey. I'll take care of you while you're growing up, and teach you everything I know so one day you can be the best rancher in the state of Wyoming."

"And can I ride Geronimo again?" Joey asked, hugging Hawk with his small arms.

"As long as I'm with you. One day, when you're big enough, you can ride him by yourself."

"In a decade, maybe." Amanda rose to her feet but before she could take a step away, Hawk encircled her waist and drew her into his embrace. She looked up, a question in her eyes.

"Seems like we're going to be a family," he said softly. He bent and kissed her lightly, kissed Joey on the cheek and let the squirming child down, chuckling as Joey wiped his cheek.

"I don't like mushy stuff," he complained. "Can I go tell everybody?"

"Sure," Hawk agreed, his arm still around Amanda. "Pepe and Jeremy know but you can tell everyone else."

Her confusion showed on her face. "Now what's the problem?" he asked.

"I'm still wondering if we're doing the right thing," she replied.

"Don't worry about it, sugar. It'll work out. We're going into this with our eyes open. You have something I want, I can give you something you want. It'll work, you'll see."

She pulled away and headed out of the office. She wanted some time to herself. It was happening too fast and as much as she wanted to be married, doubts were building about the chances of a successful marriage without a strong foundation of love.

"Amanda?"

"I'm going to fix dinner." She didn't stop, didn't turn around. She wanted to be alone.

When the men came into dinner a short time later, Walt immediately headed for Amanda.

"Is it true, what the boy said, you and Hawk are getting married?" Walt asked.

"That's right."

"Told you he'd be staying," Walt said complacently.

Amanda wished she could tell him why Hawk was staying. The men seemed happy for her. She should try to be happy, too, but the uncertainty and doubts grew stronger. She wasn't at all certain she knew what she was doing.

"We want you to come to the wedding. It'll be on Friday, in town."

"In Tagget?" Walt asked.

"That's right." She tilted her chin. "Any reason it shouldn't be?"

"None." He smiled. "I'm pleased to be invited. I'll be there for sure."

"I will be there, too," Pepe agreed. "You want the new men, as well?"

She hesitated, glanced over to see Matt and Jeremy standing by their chairs, their eyes on her.

"Yes. Everyone who is a part of the Royal Flush is invited."

"Congratulations, ma'am," Matt said. "Mind if I bring Karen?"

"Oh. I guess not." So much for her original thought that she and Hawk would slip into some judge's chambers and have a quick ceremony. This was sounding more and more like a real wedding.

Which it was, of course. Legal and binding. Only the circumstances surrounding it were a bit odd.

"Congratulations, Hawk," Matt called when Hawk entered the kitchen.

He grinned, his eyes going to Amanda's.

"You take good care of this little gal," Walt admonished. "She's like family to me and Pepe. You give her any grief, you'll have to answer to us, boy."

Hawk nodded, his expression solemn. "I'll take care of her, Walt."

"I know you will. She's a good woman."

"You're right."

"So when's the wedding?" Jeremy asked once they were all seated.

"Friday at ten at the Presbyterian Church."

"Not one to let the grass grow under your feet once you make up your mind, are you?" Pepe asked with a grin.

"Nope, no reason to wait, is there, sugar?" Hawk asked.

She shook her head, glad he'd not told the rest of them the real reason for their hasty marriage. She would hate for it to get back to the Pembrokes that she was marrying only to settle the custody suit.

And so she told him later that night. They were in her room, undressing, when she stopped and looked at him.

"I appreciate your not telling anyone about the custody battle, or the reason for our marriage," she said.

"Nobody's business but our own. You can't keep the custody suit a secret forever, though. Once the county starts sending the people who are investigating the Pembroke charges, everyone will know."

She sighed, walking over to the window to look out. It was dark, the night sky filled with stars. The moon was a small crescent on the horizon. "I guess."

He came up behind her and rested his hands on her shoulders, drawing her back against his chest. He'd already removed his shirt, and she felt the heat from his bare skin. And she felt his strength. He was a man she could lean on when things got too tough. And he cared for Joey.

"It'll work out, sugar. I promised you that."

"It's not fair, you know," she said slowly. "Bobby Jack wanted nothing to do with Joey. Now that he's gone, it's not fair that his parents think they can waltz in and take over."

"No, it's not fair. But we'll deal with it, and make it come right. Stop worrying."

"I can't." She glared at him. "None of this would be happening if you hadn't taken Joey into town when I said not to," she said bitterly.

Hawk shrugged. "True. And you have every right to be angry. But, Amanda, I'm doing all I can to make it up to you. Put your anger on hold for a while. Let's see what happens, can we?" He turned her around and cupped her face in his callused hands. "I will not let them take Joey from you," he promised.

Heat enveloped her. Reluctantly, almost as if unable to help herself, she reached out her fingers and trailed them across his shoulders, dropping under his arms to trace them across the muscles of his chest. She rubbed one tight nipple, enchanted with the swift indrawn breath.

"Two can play this game, sugar," he said, rubbing his thumb against her collarbone, slipping beneath the opening in her shirt to touch her soft warm skin.

"I like this game," she whispered as she leaned into him for a kiss.

For a few dazzling moments anger and fear and uncertainty with the custody battle fled as she gave herself up to the pleasure only this man could bring. His touch inflamed her, his lips drew a response she didn't know she could give. By the time their clothes had been shed and they were holding on tightly to each other in the narrow bed, she had forgotten all her worries. She could only feel the man in her arms, feel the shimmering tension build, feel the glorious release his lovemaking brought.

In the cooling aftermath, she almost dozed off, but there was something she wanted to say. "Hawk?"

"Hmmm?" He sounded sleepy.

"I thought you wanted a baby," she murmured, relishing the feeling of his chest against her breasts, his hair-roughened legs tangled with hers, the sleek skin beneath her hands as she clung to his back. She wished the nights were hours longer. She hated to be parted, even for the few hours of the day.

"I do. What do you want, another little boy or a little girl?"

"I don't care. Why did you use the condom, then?" If they had a child would it insure he'd stay?

He pulled back a little, and smoothed her hair back from her face. "I wanted to wait."

"For what?" Uncertainty rose again. Was he going to make sure he could stand marriage before committing to a child?

"For our wedding night."

Once again he surprised her. "Hawk, I have to tell you, I think you have a romantic streak I never suspected."

"Not me, sugar," he protested, his hands still smoothing through her hair, his fingers rubbing the silky strands.

"It does clash with your image, but I think it's there."

"I don't care for the mushy stuff, as Joey says."

"I thought you liked kisses."

He covered her mouth with his in a deep kiss. When they came up for air, he rubbed her lips with his thumb. "I like your kisses."

"That's mushy stuff." She liked his kisses, more than she thought she should. One kiss from him and everything flew out of her brain. She had to work to keep some semblance of coherence. Even though they'd just made love, even though he'd just kissed her senseless, she desired more.

"That kind of mushy stuff I like. It's talk about romance and love and all that that I don't like."

"All right, I won't say any more." But she would be watching. Sometimes the things a person did spoke louder than words. And she was secretly charmed that this rough, hard-looking fistfighting cowboy might have a romantic streak a mile wide.

"Did I tell you Alec confirmed he's coming?" Hawk said, settling her down and drawing up the sheet.

"Yes, and Mitzy. Did you ask your father?"

"No. He would not add to the festive atmosphere. Did you ask your mother?"

"No." She hadn't even told her mother. The woman hadn't contacted her in more than five years. She obviously didn't care. Maybe one day she'd drop her a card and let her know. And then again maybe she wouldn't. While her mother had never let her go hungry or unclothed, neither had she ever showed her the love Amanda showered on her son. Her mother had been too interested in the next man on the horizon to care for her own daughter.

"So we build a better family than either of us had," Hawk said, as if divining her thoughts.

"Yes, I'd like that."

Eleven

Amanda stood inside the boutique feeling awkward and totally out of place. She had never shopped in a boutique before. When she'd shopped with her mother years ago, they'd gone to the local department store. More recently she had bought her jeans and shirts from a catalog. She'd never even been in such an exclusive shop.

When the saleswoman came up to them, Amanda felt clumsy and unkempt. The woman personified sleek sophisticated perfection. She wore a red suit that fit her as if made exclusively for her, plunging in front, with an indecently short skirt. Her hair was carefully tousled and her makeup artfully applied. Though discreet, her glance had obviously summed up Amanda and then dismissed her. Not surprising considering Amanda wore faded jeans, a cotton shirt and had her hair braided down her back.

The saleswoman turned, instead, to Hawk, her glance running appreciatively over him.

"How can I help you today?" she asked. Even her voice sounded sophisticated and sharp. No western drawl there.

"Looking for a dress. A wedding dress," Hawk said smoothly.

"Mommy and Daddy are getting married." Joey peeked around Amanda at the woman. He'd been promised his ice-cream cone if he behaved at the store.

Hawk smiled down at the woman. He held his hat in one hand, the other firmly gripped Amanda's shoulder. "That's right."

Does he think I'll bolt if he doesn't hold me? Amanda wondered. The thought crossed her mind. She didn't belong here. This store was way out of her league.

The saleswoman looked nonplussed for a moment, then her business sense took over. "How nice. Are you the bride?" she asked Amanda, skimming her eyes over her again.

"Yes." She wanted to leave. She didn't need this.

"I'm Alison Towers, I manage this place. We don't really carry wedding dresses, I'm afraid."

"I just want a nice dress. It's not a formal wedding," Amanda said, standing taller. If Hawk didn't block the door, she would have left by now.

"It's a morning wedding, Friday," Hawk volunteered.

"I see." Alison nodded and turned toward a rack. "I think we can find something."

"Something pretty," Hawk said firmly.

"I'm sure it will be nice, Hawk," Amanda whispered. "Why don't you and Joey wait outside."

"Not until I see the dress," he said.

"I can be trusted to buy a dress."

"Nothing practical? Nothing that you can wear around the house?" he asked.

"For heaven's sake, Hawk, this is my wedding dress. And I don't wear dresses around the house."

"Right, you don't even own one."

"Shhh." Amanda glanced over at the saleswoman, but she apparently hadn't heard, or was smart enough to ignore the bit of information.

"You could wait in the truck for me."

"We're not waiting in the truck. Joey and I will wander around town while you're here, if you like."

She wanted to protest, wanted to tell him to keep Joey close, to make sure the Pembrokes couldn't—

"I'll watch him, but we're not staying in the truck," Hawk said firmly.

"Okay, I won't be long."

"Meet us at the ice-cream shop." He put his hat on. "Let's go, Joey. This kind of shopping is for women, not men."

"Great, now you're teaching him sexist attitudes so he grows up to be some dumb macho cowboy who thinks—"

Hawk reached around her neck and drew her against him, pressing his mouth against hers to shut her up. When she pulled back, glaring at him, he smiled.

"Never once heard you complain about me being a dumb macho cowboy."

"Well, just because you haven't heard..." she trailed off, looking at the lips that had kissed her. She wished they were alone so she could have another kiss. Another of his melt-your-toes kisses.

"Oh, go on, the two of you. I'll get a dress and meet you at the ice-cream shop," she said, turning back to head toward the rack the saleswoman rummaged through.

The truth was, there wasn't a thing she would change about Hawk even if she could. Her eyes followed him as he walked through the dainty dress shop. He'd never looked so masculine as he did surrounded by lace and silk and women's fashion.

"Almost makes me forget I'm happily married," Alison said, walking toward Amanda with two dresses over her arm.

Amanda turned and smiled shyly. "He's quite something, isn't he?"

"And you're crazy about him, just as he is."

Amanda nodded, her eyes going to the dresses.

"I think this one is great, and would be perfect with your slender height." Alison held up one dress, a creamy concoction of silk with a full skirt and a softly draped bodice. "Or there's this one, but it's a bit more fussy." Lace and silk and dressy. Both were beautiful.

"I don't know."

"Well, let's try them on."

The next half hour Amanda tried on clothes, underwear and shoes. She bought the first dress, the creamy silk. It caressed her body when she moved, making her feel like a queen. Alison had talked her into the most daring underwear, more lace and air than anything she'd ever seen before. Sheer thigh-top stockings and elegant silk shoes finished her ensemble.

"What are you going to do about a hat or veil?" Alison asked as she wrapped the items in tissue before putting them in a bag.

"I don't know, I hadn't thought about it. I guess just curl my hair." She hadn't fussed with her hair in years. A braid suited ranch life. Now she'd have to hope she could remember how to curl it and make it look presentable.

Alison rang up the total, lost in thought. Finally she looked at Amanda. "I had a hat when I married Charlie. It's white, though it's aged a bit since we've been married so it's almost the same color as this dress. Enough of a match that it wouldn't look out of place. I still have it if you would like to borrow it for the wedding."

Amanda stared at her. She had met the woman a half hour ago and she was offering to lend her her wedding hat?

"I don't—"

"Now don't worry about it, it would finish your look. You want to be beautiful and look like a bride for him, don't you?"

It's our only wedding. Hawk's words echoed in her mind. She did want to be beautiful, if only for a morning. She didn't ever want him to regret marrying her.

"Thank you. If you're sure you don't mind, I'd like to borrow it."

"Great. Shall I run it by your place later?"

"I live out of town on a ranch. Maybe I could just pick it up the morning of the wedding."

"Sure. I could bring it to the church if you like."

They discussed it for a few minutes, agreeing in the end that Alison would bring it to the church, and stay for the ceremony.

Amanda left the shop, looking to the left and right. She saw a couple of people she knew, but they didn't notice her. She had waited in vain for any censure from Alison once she discovered her name. Maybe she didn't know who Amanda was. And it had been fun shopping, with another woman to advise her. If she ever had the need for a dress again, she would come back.

"We made it," Hawk said as he pulled the truck away from the curb later.

"Made what?" she asked, holding her packages in her lap. She didn't want the dress crushed.

"Didn't run into anyone who had a bad word to say to either of us."

She nodded, glancing at Joey.

"Did you get a pretty dress?"

"I think so."

"You can show me when we get home."

"No, it's bad luck to see the dress before the wedding. We have enough against us without bad luck."

"Nothing's against us, sugar. We've the world by the tail."

She shook her head and looked out the window. What would happen if things didn't go the way Hawk predicted? What if the Pembrokes were successful in getting custody of Joey? Would Hawk stay after that? There would no longer be any need. And what would she do then?

"Hey."

She looked up.

"You're worrying again. Stop."

She nodded, knowing she couldn't.

"We went into the restaurant and looked around, Mommy," Joey said.

"Joey, that was to be a secret," Hawk said with some amusement.

"You said the party was the secret," Joey said, looking up at Hawk trustingly.   .

Hawk grimaced and shot a glance at Amanda.

"What party?" she asked warily.

"Reception, actually. I reserved one of the banquet rooms at the Pines."

"Hawk, that's the most expensive place in town."

"Relax, part of the wedding."

"Well, the bride is supposed to pay for the wedding and—"

"Except when the groom does. Damn, *groom.* It still doesn't feel real."

"It feels more than real to me. I just bought a wedding dress."

"Which you won't let me see before Friday morning."

"Oh, Walt or Pepe will have to drive me in. You'll have to go with Matt or Jeremy. You can't see me before the ceremony," she said suddenly.

"Hell, does that mean I have to spend tomorrow night in the bunkhouse?"

She glared at him, then nodded toward Joey who watched the adults talk.

"Yes."

Hawk chuckled. "Guess one more night won't kill me." But he wondered if it would. He was used to sleeping with Amanda after only a couple of nights. God, he was getting in deep. But he knew where he was going. He knew what he was doing. He would make sure the Pembrokes had no case, take care of

Amanda and Joey and gain interest in a ranch. And his marriage would be different than his father's!

After dinner that night Hawk sent Joey to watch TV with Walt and pulled Amanda out of the kitchen and to the front porch. He sat on the swing and pulled her into his lap.

"Now, Amanda, I want to do this right. Will you marry me?"

She nodded. "I thought we had already decided that," she said, puzzled.

"Yes or no, not just a nod."

"Yes, Hawk, I would be most honored to marry you," she said formally.

"Good." He eased her back a little and reached into his front pocket. Withdrawing a diamond ring, he held out his hand for hers.

Amanda felt the prick of tears as she laid her left hand in his. In seconds, he slipped the engagement ring on her finger, raised her hand and kissed her palm. And the man said he didn't have a romantic notion in him, she thought, touched beyond belief.

"Oh, Hawk," she said, raising her hand to see the sparkling diamond from the light in the house. The solitary setting was beautiful, the diamond large. The band fit perfectly. "It's lovely," she whispered, blinking quickly, lest the tears that threatened spilled over. She could never explain that to him.

"I hoped you would like it." He hugged her closer and kissed her cheek. She turned and her mouth found his. The kiss was long, sweet and gentle. Her heart beat heavily in her chest. Maybe things would work out for them. If it did not, it would not be because of lack of trying on her part. She would cherish this moment for years to come. Probably forever. If he loved her, it would be perfect. But she couldn't expect everything.

The next night Amanda had butterflies. She kept looking at Hawk as they all ate dinner. She could scarcely believe that by dinner tomorrow she'd be married. And to this rugged, sexy cowboy. She didn't know anything about being married. Her mother had not been married, nor had Jonas or Walt or Pepe. Maybe she should just sell Hawk the ranch and take Joey and disappear. She could move to another state where the Pembrokes would never find them.

Taking a deep breath, she tried to calm down. She was panicking for no reason. Nothing drastic was going to happen. She and Hawk were already sleeping together; the only difference would be they would now use the big bed in the master bedroom, which she had cleaned thoroughly that morning.

She supposed Hawk would take over the direction of the cattle operation on the ranch. Which wasn't all bad. That would leave her to concentrate on her beloved quarter horses.

And he was good to Joey. She didn't see that changing.

And she loved him. She didn't see that changing, ever.

Hawk covered her fingers. She focused on him.

"You okay?" he asked softly.

She nodded.

He studied her face for a few moments, then nodded and squeezed her fingers before releasing them. She felt his touch long after he resumed eating. It warmed her entire body.

"Come to town with us, Hawk. We'll celebrate your last night of being a free man," Jeremy invited.

"No thanks, I'll pass this time."

"You have to have a last fling," Matt protested.

Hawk shook his head, glancing at Amanda. "Last time I celebrated something I ended up in a fight, fired and kicked out. I don't dare risk it again."

She smiled, remembering the day she'd met him. He'd been bruised and aching. But he had stood up for her, even on that first day.

"Besides, I'm moving my stuff in tonight," he said casually.

"We could help," Walt said.

"Trying to kick me out, eh?"

"We know you won't want to waste any time tomorrow with moving and such," Pepe replied, his eyes twinkling.

Amanda felt the flush of embarrassment and looked at her plate. All the men laughed. Her lips twitched, but she refused to meet any eye.

"I can help, too, Hawk," Joey said. "I mean, Daddy."

"Good, partner, I could use it."

When Amanda went to bed that night, she couldn't sleep. It wasn't just the prewedding jitters. She missed Hawk. They had only started spending the nights together a few days ago, but she had grown used to being crowded in her single bed. Now she missed his warmth, his solid strength holding her.

Lying on her back, she gazed out of the window at the stars. It had been odd moving all her things into Jonas's old room. Even odder when Hawk and Walt and Jeremy had started bringing in his clothes and putting them in the closet next to her jeans, in the drawers, next to her things.

Hawk had done the dresser, and paused a couple of times, his hands touching her clothes. She smiled at the erotic thoughts that chased around in her mind. There was something very sexy about a big rugged outdoorsman touching a woman's things. She hoped he liked the dress she'd chosen to wear tomorrow, and the sinful underwear she would wear beneath it.

Finally, exhausted, she drifted to sleep, imagining Hawk's expression when he took off her dress tomorrow night.

Twelve

Her wedding day! Amanda was scared to her toes. She didn't know whether to call it off or go through with it. When Joey bounded into her room before she was even up, she welcomed him into her bed and snuggled down with him. He was so precious to her. His little-boy scent filled her, his unconditional love and devotion warmed her as nothing ever had. She had been truly blessed to have such a sweet child. And she would do anything to protect him. Even marry a man who didn't love her.

"After today I'll be sleeping in Jonas's room with Hawk," she explained.

"Is he going to stay forever and ever?" Joey asked.

"Yes." At least she hoped he would.

"So I will stay with him now instead of you?"

"Oh, no, Joey. Sweetheart, you will stay with me. We'll just have Hawk stay with us, as well."

"He said I was to give you away. I didn't want to give you away, Mommy, but Hawk said to."

She laughed and hugged him closer. "Joey, what Hawk meant was you are to walk with me in the church and say it's okay if I marry him. But I'm not leaving you—I would never leave you."

He smiled. "I'm glad. I love you."

"I love you, too, Joey."

Amanda dressed calmly, belying the inner tension. She curled her hair, drew it back from her face and let it fall to midback. She applied makeup sparingly, but was pleased with the result. Anyone looking at her would know in an instant that she loved the man she was marrying. Well, so what? It was true. She wasn't ashamed of it. Just afraid to let him know. It was not part of their deal.

She donned the lacy underwear, feeling decadent and indescribably sexy. She had never worn sheer stockings before. Drawing them on, she arched her foot. Her legs were nice. She hoped Hawk thought so.

Finally she lowered the dress over her head and zipped it up. It fit as though it had been made especially for her. The ivory tint enhanced her own coloring. For several moments she stared at herself, almost not recognizing the reflection. Slowly she smiled. She did look pretty.

Walt and Pepe were waiting in the hall when she came down the stairs. They both wore suits, cowboy boots shined to a high sheen and their best hats.

"Well, don't you look a picture," Walt said gruffly.

"Amanda, honey, you look a treat. I wish Jonas

could be here to see you," Pepe said, his lined face smiling broadly.

"I wish he were here, too. I miss him," she said, touched at the reception by her two old friends.

"He always loved you, honey. Just as we do. He wanted you to be happy. I reckon he'd like Hawk even if he might not have thought him good enough for you. But we'll keep him in line for you."

"Yes, boss. If you ever need anything, you know you can count on Walt and me," Pepe said.

"Thank you," she said gravely. Hugging them in turn, she felt her eyes fill with tears. "Here we are getting all sentimental and we've got a wedding to get to. Don't you make me cry and ruin my makeup."

"Naw, just wanted you to know."

She nodded and turned to call Joey. In minutes they were squeezed into Walt's old Ford and heading for Tagget.

Alison Towers stood outside the church with a tall deputy sheriff. For a second Amanda's heart caught. The Pembrokes hadn't sent someone for Joey, had they? Mitzy said Amanda could keep Joey unless the custody hearing went against her.

When Walt stopped the car in front of the steps, Alison hurried over to greet Amanda, the deputy following.

"I'll park and be right in," Walt said as the others climbed out.

"Hi," Alison said.

"Hi. Thanks for coming."

"You do look nice. There's a room off the foyer that we can use to finish getting ready. Hi, Joey."

"Hi." He half hid behind Amanda, watching the deputy walk toward them.

"Amanda, I'd like you to meet Charlie, my husband. Charlie, this is Amanda. Oh, dear, I don't even know your last name."

"Well, for the next few minutes it's Williams, but after that it will be Blackstone."

"We're marrying Hawk," Joey said. "Is that a real gun?"

Charlie smiled and nodded. "Not for show-and-tell."

"Wow." Joey's eyes grew big as he studied the gun.

"Let's go inside. It's almost ten. And I wouldn't want to keep that hunk you're marrying waiting," Alison said. "Is it all right if Charlie comes with us?"

"Sure," Amanda agreed. The more the merrier.

In less than two minutes Alison declared herself satisfied with Amanda's appearance. The picture-book hat completed the bridal look. For a long moment Amanda gazed at the mirror. She would do Hawk proud.

"Here, Hawk asked me to make sure you got this." Alison handed her a large white box. "I'm going out now to sit down. I'll let the organist know you're ready."

"Organist?"

"To accompany your walk down the aisle." Alison gave her a cheery wave and disappeared into the sanctuary.

Amanda opened the box. Inside nestled a bridal bouquet.   Tears flooded her eyes.

"What's the matter, Mommy? Are you hurted?" Joey asked.

"I think your mother is turning into a mushy old woman." Slowly she lifted out the bouquet of white roses and baby's breath. Long creamy ribbons trailed down before her. She held the flowers before her waist. She was a bride!

"Let's get this show on the road, Joey. Ready to go marry Hawk?"

"Yes!"

She took her son's hand in hers and waited for the music. Hearing the familiar tune, she smiled tremulously and started down the aisle toward Hawk.

The church seemed full. Then she realized it was just the friends they had invited. Mitzy had agreed to be her witness and stood as a bridesmaid in a lovely dark rose suit. The tall man beside Hawk must be his brother. She saw Walt and Pepe in pews right up front on the left. Matt, Karen and Jeremy sat on the right. Alison and her husband sat behind them. She had not expected so many.

Hawk wore a dark gray suit, shockingly white shirt and blue-and-silver tie. His hair was combed, his cowboy hat not in evidence. He stood tall and proud and watched her every step.

God, she was beautiful. With her shiny chestnut hair curled and hanging down her back, she made him think of their nights in bed, with that soft silky hair spread around. Her dress fit like a dream, showing off her slender curves and long legs. He gulped.

When he looked into her eyes, they blazed with some emotion he couldn't define. But she looked happy, and for that he was grateful. He wanted her happy. No matter what, he vowed to keep her happy.

Amanda stepped beside him, and smiled.

He took her hand and pressed a man's ring into her palm. She closed her eyes for a second. She'd forgotten that. Thankfully he had not. Nodding briefly, she turned her attention to Reverend Patterson and the familiar words he recited.

When the man asked who gave the woman, Amanda looked at Joey and reached down to squeeze his hand slightly. He smiled up at her and then at the preacher.

"It's all right for my mommy to marry Hawk," he said loud and clear.

The congregation laughed.

Hawk reached down and took Joey's other hand. "Thanks, partner," he said softly.

The ceremony went without a flaw. When it came time to kiss the bride, Hawk tilted her chin with his finger and kissed her warmly. Joey tugged on his hand.

"That's mushy stuff again," he complained.

"I think I'm hooked on mushy stuff," Hawk said for Amanda's ear alone, then straightened and turned to face their friends.

Amanda had her engagement ring such a short time, she had not gotten used to it. Now she had a gold band beside it. She studied her hand as Hawk drove the pickup truck toward the ranch. The fragrance of her bouquet filled the cab. The day was warm and the air stirred her curls. She'd returned Alison's hat. But she still felt like a bride in her dress.

It had been a wonderful day. She had met and liked Hawk's brother, Alec. Alison and her husband, residents of Tagget for less than two years, had been a delightful addition to the wedding group. They had already made plans to invite them to the ranch one Sunday. Despite her sophisticated appearance, Alison insisted she would love to help out on a ranch for a day or two.

Mitzy had stayed long enough to eat, then claimed she had to get back to work. She pulled Amanda aside before leaving and told her she thought the marriage would put an end to any hope the Pembrokes had of custody.

And Hawk had been beside her almost every moment, touching her hand, trailing his fingers through her long hair while he talked to his brother, or Charlie Towers, playing with her fingers while he traded jokes with Jeremy and Pepe. His hand had held hers while they chatted with Matt and Karen. And he made sure his palm covered her hand as she cut the small wedding cake the restaurant had provided. The only time he hadn't been right by her, he'd been talking with Matt and Walt and his brother Alec.

All in all a wonderful day. She sighed.

"Tired?"

"A bit. Everything went well, don't you think?"

"Were you expecting something to go wrong?"

"I thought maybe the Pembrokes would do something to stop the wedding, or make an attempt to see Joey," she admitted.

"I almost wish they had," he murmured.

"What?"

"I would have loved an excuse to beat him to a pulp."

She giggled. "While I wouldn't mind, I hardly think I want my new husband to spend our wedding night in jail."

"So you might notice if I wasn't in bed tonight?"

"I might. I missed you last night," she said softly.

"Probably not as much as I missed you, sugar.

Since Walt and Pepe are watching Joey tonight, and they're all staying in town until after dinner, we have the ranch to ourselves for a while.''

"Great, all those chores, just the two of us," she teased.

"I was thinking more of that brand-new bed, and just the two of us."

"There is that," she said.

When Hawk stopped the truck by the kitchen door, he put his hand on her arm. "Wait there," he said.

He went around the truck and opened her door, scooping her up into his arms.

"Well, Mrs. Blackstone, welcome home." He started for the back stairs.

"Are you carrying me over the threshold?" she asked, delighted.

"Tradition, isn't it?"

"Yes." She smiled and held on, her bouquet in one hand, her other clutching his shoulder.

He carried her over the threshold, through the kitchen and up the stairs to the big corner room. Stopping beside the new bed, he lowered her feet to the floor.

"Did I thank you for the flowers?" she asked, suddenly shy. "They are beautiful."

He took them from her and tossed them to a chair. "You are beautiful. My heart almost stopped when you started walking down that aisle," he growled, lowering his head to kiss her.

The flare of attraction between them grew stronger than ever. Instantly every fiber of her being yearned for his touch, his kisses, the special magic that claimed her whenever he was around. Lost in his embrace, she gave everything to the man who was now her husband.

Hawk slid his hands over her back, impatient with the barrier of clothing. He sought and found the zipper. Slowly he slid it down. When he eased the dress off her shoulders, he stopped and stared at the lacy confection covering her breasts.

"Oh, my, are you trying to drive me crazy?" he asked, his fingertips brushing against the edge of the lace.

Slowly Amanda smiled. "I bought a lot of fancy underwear," she said seductively.

He groaned and lowered his mouth to cover one impudent nipple pressing saucily against the feminine covering.

She gripped his shoulders, her mind spinning in a thousand directions as her pulse rate soared.

When he slipped the dress over her hips and let it pool on the floor, he stopped, and leaned his forehead against hers. "Mrs. Blackstone, do you know how many times I've wanted to put my hands on you when you were strutting around the yard?" His callused palms covered her bottom, bringing her to nestle against the hard ridge of his desire. "Do you know how many times I've wanted to drag you behind the barn and make love until the sun rose?"

Amanda stared at him, amazed. "Hawk." She put her fingers over his lips, brushing against his hard jaw. No one had ever desired her that way. He was so different from the cowboys in town who had propositioned her for years. Her toes curled and she gave herself up to his touch.

Impatiently, he scooped her up and placed her on

the mattress. He made quick work of stripping the remainder of his clothes from his body.

Amanda stared, her heart pounding, heat pouring through her at the sight of his desire for her. She cleared her throat, trying to find the words, but none came before he covered her body and kissed her long and hard. His hands combed through her hair as if savoring the silky feel of each strand. His legs spread hers and slowly he eased into her.

Rising up just a bit, he looked down at her, cupping her face in his hands. "Tell me what you want, and I'll do my best to get it for you," he said.

Her hands clutched his arms. She knew he felt guilty for exposing Joey. She knew he had not planned to stay, but had wanted to move on when he found his ranch. She didn't understand. Though the hope began to blossom deep within her.

She swallowed, unable to look away. Unable to still the roiling sensations that were building deep within her as he slowly moved back and forth. Tears filled her eyes.

"I didn't know…" She blinked furiously but couldn't stem the flow of tears.

"Oh, sugar, don't cry." He kissed her frantically, as if trying to stop the flow that way. She reacted as she always had and in only seconds they were blazing again. Cresting the heights of passion, affirmation and desire bound them together as they exploded over the summit together.

Amanda relaxed and savored the feel of his heavy body covering hers. Her hands traced the muscles of his back, relishing the sensations with her fingertips.

"That's done," he murmured, kissing her neck.

"What's done?" she asked.

"Our marriage is now consummated," he said with deep satisfaction.

"That's why we rushed home, just to consummate the union?" she asked, pushing him away so she could see his face.

Slowly Hawk rolled to his side, bringing her with him. He stroked back the hair from her face and looked down into her eyes.

"I wanted everything settled," he said.

"Why?"

"To be sure."

She stared at him, love growing and spilling over into every cell of her body. He had been uncertain about her? He had married her to protect Joey, and wanted to make certain everything was settled. She had never felt so cherished in her life. She wished she could share her feelings with him, but something held her back. He'd never asked for love. Never expressed any love for her. She dare not say anything. Not yet.

Not until things were clear with Joey.

Thirteen

Amanda couldn't believe the changes the next two weeks brought. Hawk called old rodeo buddies who showed up ready to work. The house and barn were repainted, the corral replaced. With four more ranch hands, the work became easily spread around, easily handled, though the cooking had increased. Amanda spent more time at the house and less out on the range. It gave her time to spend with Joey. She bought him a pony for his birthday and spent hours teaching him how to ride and how to care for the pony. They had a quiet family celebration—all the men chipping in to give Joey the saddle and bridle for his new pony.

The county social worker had been by. Joey's testing had proved outstanding, the results well ahead of grade level. The social worker had commented on how happy and well adjusted the boy was. And how well run the ranch appeared.

Still they heard nothing from the attorney.

Watching Joey ride his pony around the corral, Amanda couldn't help wonder where they were heading. Each night Hawk made love to her. And never once used protection. Was he planning to stay forever? She hoped so, but couldn't plan on anything until she knew the fate of her son's future.

When the phone rang, she answered it from the barn. It was Mitzy.

"They've withdrawn the custody suit," she said without preamble. "Your husband apparently made it clear they had no chance of winning and a trial would result in smearing Bobby Jack's name from one end of the state to the other. Mrs. Pembroke would not stand for that. They do not want to discuss visitation."

Amanda's knees gave way and she sank down on the barn floor. "He's mine?" The relief was overwhelming. Tears coursed down her cheeks. The fear disappeared. She had her son.

"Mitzy, thank you," she whispered. She listened, astonished, as the lawyer disclaimed any part in what had happened. Listened in astonishment at the things Mitzy had to say.

Amanda sat on the new corral railing a half hour later watching Joey ride Patches when she heard the horses. Jumping down, she began to run toward Hawk, her face beaming.

"He's mine. They withdrew the complaint," she yelled as he rode toward her. Spurring his horse, in only seconds he drew up beside her, reaching down to pull her up before him on the saddle.

"What are you yelling about?" he asked, grinning at the wide smile on her face.

"Joey's all mine. The Pembrokes withdrew their suit!" Joy almost bubbled out of her. "Hawk, you did it, just like you promised. There's no more lawsuit!"

"That's great."

"And that's not all," she said as the other cowboys rode by, touching the brim of their hats when she beamed at each one.

"Well?"

Once the others had moved on toward the barn, she looked at Hawk sternly. "I understand from Mitzy that the entire town was on my side. Someone had started a series of rumors against the Pembrokes. And someone else had started questioning my reputation, trying to pinpoint anyone who had ever dated me. And they could only find Jeff Morgan, and that was when we were in junior high."

Hawk nudged his horse, turning away from the house and walking slowly toward the hills. "Now how could that have happened?"

"You did that, too, didn't you? Threatened the Pembrokes. Then the whole town?" She cupped his face and kissed him hard. "Thank you, you gave me my son."

"No, sugar. They would never have gotten him. I promised you, remember? Besides, it made sense that if Bobby Jack had lied about Joey being his son, he'd lied about all the rest. It was easy to prove that once people began talking."

She nodded, suddenly aware they were moving away from the house.

"Where are we going?" she asked.

"I want to talk to you," he said seriously.

Fear clutched her heart. She didn't want to talk

about anything. She wanted to relish the freedom of fear about Joey, not worry Hawk was going to tell her something she didn't want to hear.

Was he going to tell her he was leaving? The reason for their marriage had now passed. Maybe his real estate agent had found a ranch he could get, one that didn't need a ton of work to bring it up to scratch.

"I should get back to Joey," she said, wanting to postpone hearing what Hawk had to say.

"There are nine men there, surely between them they can keep an eye out for the boy."

Wiping her damp palms against her jeans, she tried to pull away from him, but the way he had placed her on the saddle, she didn't have much maneuvering room.

"What do you want to talk about?" she asked. Taking a deep breath, she tried to clamp down on her emotions. She could do this. If he wanted to leave, she'd be calm. She would not create a scene. He had helped her out and she would always be beholden to him for that. Not that he wanted gratitude. But she would ask for nothing—

"I spoke to Tom Standish today," he said.

"What?" That had been the last thing she had expected.

"Yeah. Told him I was interested in buying some of his land if he was interested in selling."

"You told him what?" She stared at him over her shoulder. For a moment the irony of the situation threatened to make her laugh. "He tried to run me off so he could get my ranch and you told him you wanted part of his?"

"Yes." Hawk raised an eyebrow. "You have a problem with that?"

She giggled. "No. I wish I could have seen Tom's face."

"Well, he did look a bit surprised."

"What did he say?"

"Hell would freeze over first." Hawk shrugged. "So next we hit up your other neighbors. One day someone might be interested in selling a few acres."

She gazed around, unsure just what to say. "So you're staying?"

"Staying where?"

"Here?"

"What do you mean?" He pulled the horse to a halt, lifted her down and dismounted.

She took a deep breath. "Are you staying on the Royal Flush with me and Joey? I mean the danger is gone, now that the Pembrokes pulled back. And I know you travel from place to place, and wanted a ranch of your own."

Anger flared. "Are you telling me to take a hike?" he asked, his hands balling at his sides.

"No." She recognized the danger signs. "No, Hawk. I don't want you to leave, ever."

"Then what are you talking about?"

"I know you married me to help keep Joey."

His fist came up beneath her chin and he tilted her face up to his. Brushing his mouth against hers, he shook his head. "You know damn all, sugar. I married you because I wanted you. And now that I have you, I will never let you go."

She could hardly breathe. Taking a chance, she said, "Sounds almost like love to me."

"Sounds like love to me," he repeated, his eyes holding hers as astonishment showed in his gaze.

She blinked. "Hawk?"

He gazed deep into her eyes. "What is there not to love? Do you think I would marry a woman who doesn't own a dress, buy into some dilapidated ranch, fight an entire town, for someone I don't love? What have the last few weeks been about, sugar? Sex games?"

Slowly she shook her head. "I married you because I love you," she said clearly.

He started. "Oh, sugar," he said as he pulled her tightly against him. "I think I may have loved you since I sat beside you at the diner and wished you were old enough to vote. Just took a while to sink in. I've loved you when you sashayed around the ranch with a chip on your shoulder big enough to knock you over. I love your cocky courage in standing up to the town, and your defiance to that unwarranted bad girl reputation. And I love the sweet way you deal with your son." He kissed her. "One day I want to see you deal with our children that same way."

Amanda thought her heart would burst with happiness. "I didn't know."

"Now you do. But we don't have to get all mushy about it, do we?"

She laughed. "Just a bit mushy. Especially that part about more children."

"Why do you think we need to expand the ranch? We'll need a big spread for all the kids to roam around on."

"How many are you planning?" she asked.

"As many as you want, sugar. Each one will be special, as Joey is, because they come from you."

She couldn't speak for the love that threatened to swamp her. She could only hold on to the man she loved and know that happiness would be her future, forever.

* * * * *

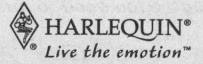

Harlequin Historicals®
Historical Romantic Adventure!

*From rugged lawmen and
valiant knights to defiant heiresses
and spirited frontierswomen,
Harlequin Historicals will
capture your imagination with
their dramatic scope, passion
and adventure.*

*Harlequin Historicals...
they're too good to miss!*

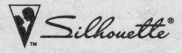

Silhouette®

SILHOUETTE *Romance*®

From first love to forever, these love stories
are fairy tale romances for today's woman.

Silhouette® *Desire*®

Modern, passionate reads that are powerful and provocative.

Silhouette® SPECIAL EDITION™

Emotional, compelling stories that capture the intensity
of living, loving and creating a family in today's world.

Silhouette® INTIMATE MOMENTS™

A roller-coaster read that delivers romantic thrills
in a world of suspense, adventure and more.